MW00966365

"Kinetic City Super Cre\

"When you want the facts—

"Megan, this is Rudy Derosa. And yes, I'd like some facts."

"Hi, Mr. Derosa," I said. "What's up?" I tried to sound cool, but in truth I felt pretty nervous. We'd never been so far from solving a case with so little time left.

"I can't believe you told the press before you told me," he said.

"Told them what?" I asked, surprised by the question.

"Told them about Boomer cheating!" Mr. Derosa replied angrily.

"What?" I asked. "We didn't say that!"

"Maybe you'll remember when I quote you," Mr. Derosa said. "Here it is. The front page of the *Kinetic City Gazette*. In a headline, no less. " 'SUPER CREW SAYS BOOMER'S THROWING THE GAMES!' "

For a moment I was stunned silent.

The Crew knew something was wrong.

"What is it, Megan?"

"What's going on?"

"What happened?"

I looked at them blankly. "Oops," I said.

KINETIC CITY super crew

Other Books in The Kinetic City Super Crew Series

Forest Slump:
The Case of the Pilfered Pine Needles
by Emily Lloyd

Hot-Tempered Farmers:
The Case of the Barbecued Barns
by Chuck Harwood

Metal Heads:
The Case of the Rival Robots
by Marianne Meyer

One Norse Town:
The Case of the Suspicious Scrolls
by J. A. Warner

Catch of the Day:
The Case of the Helpless Humpbacks
by Emily Lloyd

Tall Tales:
The Case of the Growing Suspicions
by Emily Lloyd

Rock the House:
The Case of The Meteorite Menace
by Chuck Harwood

This School Stinks!
The Case of the Secret Stench
by J.A. Warner

Home-l
Has-Bee.

The Case of the
Sluggish Slugger

Emily Lloyd

**LEARNING
TRIANGLE
PRESS**

*Connecting
kids, parents, and teachers
through learning*

An imprint of McGraw-Hill
New York San Francisco Washington, D.C. Auckland Bogotá Caracas
Lisbon London Madrid Mexico City Milan Montreal New Delhi
San Juan Singapore Sydney Tokyo Toronto

!cGraw-Hill

A Division of The **McGraw·Hill** Companies

Library of Congress Cataloging-in-Publication Data applied for.

1 2 3 4 5 6 7 8 9 0 DOC/DOC 9 0 3 2 1 0 9 8

ISBN 0-07-007066-0

The sponsoring editor for this book was Judith Terrill-Breuer, the editing supervisor was Patricia V. Amoroso, and the production supervisor was Clare B. Stanley. It was set in Century Old Style by Paul Scozzari of McGraw-Hill's Professional Book Group in Hightstown, New Jersey.

Printed and bound by R.R. Donnelley & Sons Company.

Contents

About the Crew   *vii*

About the Train   *ix*

The Phone Call   *1*

1   **The Bad-News Rockets   *3***

2   **A Day at the Park   *22***

3   **Angles in the Outfield   *34***

4   **Field of Streams   *46***

5   **Get a Clue   *53***

6   **Bats in Belfrey   *69***

7   **Let's Get Physical   *78***

8   **The Hour of our Disk-content   *92***

9   **The Rescuers   *96***

10   **Sizing up the Situation   *103***

11   **The Rockets' Red Glare   *110***

12   **Boomer Strikes Out   *116***

13   **A Special Announcement   *124***

14 Where's the Beef?   *134*

15 No Place Like Home   *140*

Get Real!   *143*

Home Crew Hands On   *148*

Puzzle Pages   *152*

Other Case Files   *163*

About the Crew

It is the near future. Peace has broken out all over the world, and the President of the United States has decided to donate the world's most sophisticated military vehicle, the X-100 Advanced Tactical Vehicle, to "the youth of America, that they might use this powerful tool to learn, to explore, and to help others."

Since the X-100 was designed in a top-secret factory in Kinetic City, the vehicle was renamed **The Kinetic City Express** and the first young crew was dubbed the **Kinetic City Super Crew**.

But who would be the members of the Crew? Kinetic City's mayor, Richard M. Schwindle, puts out a call to the young people of the city. Many answer the call, and seven are chosen: Keisha, Derek, Megan, Curtis, Fernando, PJ, and Max.

Now the Crew travel the world, along with their talkative supercomputer, ALEC, in a tireless quest for truth, justice, and the perfect deep-dish pizza. Their quest may never end.

About the Train

CIA Top-Secret Document #113057
DECLASSIFIED: 9/12/99

Originally designed to carry military intelligence teams to trouble spots throughout the world, the X-100 is capable of ultra-high-speed travel, under the control of the Advanced Logic Electronic Computer (ALEC) Series 9000. The vehicle can travel over land on existing train tracks and on tank-style treads. For crossing bodies of water, the X-100 can seal its waterproof bulkheads and travel underwater, using an advanced form of Magneto-Hydrodynamic Drive propulsion. The X-100 has several small vehicles within it which can travel with or without human passengers, including a small submarine and a jet copter. Finally, the X-100 has sophisticated information-gathering capabilities, using 'round-the-clock, high-speed access to the Internet, an extensive CD-ROM library, and the ability to generate realistic science simulations in its "Cyber Car."

The Phone Call

"Kinetic City Super Crew. When you want the facts, we hit the tracks. Megan speaking."

"Megan! This is Rudy Derosa from the Kinetic City Rockets. You gotta help me with Boomer Baxter!"

"The home-run king?"

"Ha! More like home-run has-been. He's gone bust! We're going to lose our shot at the playoffs!"

CHAPTER ONE

The Bad-News Rockets

Kinetic City Express Journal: Home-Run Has-Been:
The Case of the Sluggish Slugger. Megan reporting.
I was on hotline duty in the Control Car of the KC
Express Train the day the call came in from Rudy
Derosa. He's the manager of the Kinetic City
Rockets baseball team. We Crew members take a
lot of calls, but I'd never heard anybody sound
so desperate as Mr. Derosa when he told me all
about Boomer Baxter. Of course, he didn't really
need to tell me anything. I knew all about Boomer.
Heck, everybody in Kinetic City knew everything
about the KC Rockets' star slugger.

It all goes back to the beginning of the season.
When the Rockets started spring training this year,

they had about the same hope of winning the World Series as the Kinetic City Ballet Company did. In other words, none. The Rockets hadn't even been in a pennant race since the 1920s, before they were even called the Rockets. They were called the Stump Jumpers or something.

Anyway, right before the season started, something amazing happened. The Rockets somehow managed to trade a handful of players for the one and only Charles 'Boomer' Baxter. Boomer had spent his whole career as the star hitter for Kinetic City's arch-rival, the Blizzard Creek Hailstones, but now suddenly he was a Rocket! And from opening day right through the summer Boomer was on fire. He was on course to hit more home runs in one season than any player in history, and the rest of the Rockets team was swept right along with him.

Before long, Kinetic City was going crazy with Rockets baseball fever. The games started selling out, fan clubs were started, Boomer posters were plastered all over town. Everybody was caught up in the Boomer mania. Even I started following the Rockets, and that's saying a lot. To me, baseball was always right down there at the bottom of the Excite-O-Meter, along with watching grass grow. But this year was different. This year we had Boomer Baxter, the Home-Run King of the World!

But then, everything changed. In the last two weeks, the Rockets' record had taken a major nose-dive. They'd lost ten consecutive home games. And the reason was clear: Boomer Baxter hadn't had a single hit—much less a home run—in all those games. All Rudy Derosa needed was one more win to take his team to the playoffs. But with only three games to go and Boomer showing no signs of improvement, he was beginning to think that might not happen. That's why he called us. He needed us to get Boomer out of his slump and get the team back on track. I told Mr. Derosa that we'd get on the case right away. But when I hung up the phone, it hit me just how huge this case was. Rudy Derosa wouldn't be the only one counting on us. The entire city would be expecting us to get Boomer slugging again.

I switched on the X-100's P.A. system and paged the other Super Crew members who were on the train that day: PJ, Fernando, and Derek. A *few minutes later the Control Car doors swooshed open. PJ and Fernando walked in. Fernando was holding the remote for the Lounge Car TV high over his head, while PJ lunged at him and called him names a ninth-grader like her shouldn't know . . .*

"What's the matter, PJ?" I asked. She doesn't usually care about TV. She's too busy being a hot-shot athlete.

"Fernando wouldn't let me watch the last ten minutes of *Sports Gripe*," she explained.

Oh. That explained it. *Sports Gripe* was the local call-in show for all the city's obsessed sports fans. PJ was definitely obsessed. She was way into the Rockets even when they stunk. She knew the stats of every Rockets player all the way back to their Stump Jumper days.

"But I was trying to watch an intergalactic food fight," Fernando said. "You should see what happens to Jello in a weightless environment."

"Excuse me?" I said.

"You know, that awesome scene from episode 209 of *The Outer Edge*," Fernando explained. "It's a classic!"

"In other words," PJ said, "you've seen that same episode about twenty-three times!"

"Twenty-eight."

"But *Sports Gripe* is live!" PJ yelled.

"What's your point?" Fernando asked. I knew he was just yanking PJ's chain, but it really drove her nuts. Fernando really knew how to get PJ mad. It was just about his favorite pastime. That and watching cheezy sci-fi shows.

Just then, Derek came into the room carrying a worn-out book. He had probably been in the Library Car when I paged the Crew. Big surprise.

"It looks like the kids are getting cranky," Derek smirked as he took a seat. "Maybe it's time for their naps."

"You're hilarious, Derek," Fernando said. Derek's not that much older than us. He's a senior and Fernando and I are sophomores. And, like I said, PJ's a ninth-grader. "But I'm not the one who's cranky. PJ is."

"I am not, you Jello-brained space cadet," PJ said, sitting down angrily in a chair.

"Well, it was time to turn the TV off anyway," I said. "We've got a new case. And it's a doozy."

"You go ahead," PJ said, rolling her chair over toward the control panel. She flipped a switch and a little TV monitor built into the wall came to life.

"PJ!" I exclaimed. "This is really important!"

"I know," PJ replied, "but I *have* to hear what they're saying about Boomer."

"Boomer Baxter?" I exclaimed.

"Who else?" PJ answered.

"In that case, maybe we should all watch," I said.

"Who's Boomer Baxter?" Derek asked. He has about as much interest in sports as a dog has in catnip.

"Are you kidding me?" Fernando asked. "He's only the most talked about person in town."

But before we could explain why, PJ shushed us. The commercials were over and the show was back on the air.

HOST: "Welcome back to *Sports Gripe,* where we're always mad about something. Today we're mad about—what else—Rockets baseball. Specifically that choker, Boomer Baxter! Caller number five, you're on the air. What's your gripe?"

CALLER: "I say we send that Boomer bum back to Blizzard Creek! He makes me so mad I could spit! He's a lousy, good-for-nothin', overrated, dim-witted . . ."

HOST: "I know how you feel.

CALLER: ". . . dufus, weak-kneed, mamma's boy . . ."

HOST: "Okay! I think we get the idea. Let's move on. Caller number six, you're on *Sports Gripe*."

CALLER: "I want a refund!"

HOST: "For your tickets?"

CALLER: "For everything! My Rockets jacket, my Rockets boxer shorts, my genuine vinyl Rockets tote bag, my Boomer bath mats! I even got a Rockets tattoo!"

HOST: "Whoa. You must be bummed about that. Can you keep it covered up?"

CALLER: "I wish. But it's on my face!"

HOST: "Oops. Caller number seven? Do you have something to add?"

CALLER: ". . . worthless, lazy, no-account, stinkin' . . ."

HOST: "Well, look at the time. We gotta take another break and then we'll be right back after these messages from Rockets Hot Dogs, Rockets Root Beer, and Linda's Nail Palace, the official nail salon of Rockets baseball."

"Those people make me so mad!" PJ growled. She turned down the volume. "What is it with this town? Two weeks ago, everyone thought the Rockets were the best. Now they think they're dirt. Where's our team loyalty? Where's our city spirit? If we don't stand by our team when they're down, then how can we call ourselves fans?"

"So, PJ," I said. "How'd you like a chance to set things straight?"

"What?"

"I've been trying to tell you, that was Rudy Derosa on the phone. And he wants us to help Boomer."

"Really?" PJ said. She finally seemed interested in what I had to say. She rolled her chair over to the table.

"Would you please tell me who this Boomer guy is?" Derek asked.

"He used to be the KC Rockets' number-one hitter," PJ said. "They got him in a trade with the Blizzard Creek Hailstones at the start of the season. He's a home-run king. And he's the reason I spent three months of my allowance on these." She swung her feet up onto the table. She was wearing black sneakers with red and white stars on them.

"Cool," Fernando said.

"They're Boomer Blazers," PJ explained. "Made out of genuine recycled tires. Boomer only endorses environmentally safe products."

"So why is everyone so mad at him?" Derek asked.

"Because he hasn't had a hit in weeks," I said.

"Yeah. It's like he's a different player," PJ said.

"Maybe he is," Fernando said, his eyes lighting up. "Maybe an alien took over his body! Like in episode 116 of *The Outer Edge*! Only, maybe the alien forgot to learn how to play baseball first and . . ."

"Whoa," Derek interrupted. "I think we can safely rule out alien possession."

"I'm just kidding, Derek," Fernando said. "Besides, an alien would learn baseball in, like, two minutes. Their brains are way more advanced than ours."

Derek ignored him. "So anyway, why is this slump such a big deal?" he asked. "Lots of players go through rough spots, don't they?"

"Sure. But this is no time for a rough spot," I said. "There are only three games left in the season. If the Rockets don't win one of them, they won't make it to the playoffs."

"And without Boomer, they can't do anything," PJ added. "When he's on, the whole team gets fired up."

"And when he's off?" Fernando asked.

"The rest of them crash and burn," PJ replied.

"I can't believe one dumb jock could mess up a whole team," Derek said.

Boy, was that the wrong thing to say in front of PJ! "Who you calling a dumb jock?" she exclaimed. "Boomer happens to be brilliant! He's even got a Master's degree!"

"In what? Spitting and Scratching?" Derek replied.

"Maybe if you weren't too cool to go to a game sometime . . ."

"Okay you two, let's work together here," I said.

"So where do we start?" Fernando asked.

"I'm not sure, but the idea that Boomer's slump affects the whole team is interesting," I said. "It reminds me of this case I read about in *The National Tattler*." *The National Tattler* is my favorite newspaper, and the source of all my favorite stories. "One day, this guy in Texas started thinking he was a cow!"

"No way!" Fernando said.

"Pretty soon, the whole town thought they were cows, too."

"Really?" Fernando asked. "Did they ever get better?"

"Sure," I said. "But it was a real bummer when they had to start paying for milk again."

Fernando laughed, and even Derek cracked a half-smile. But PJ still looked sad. "I feel sorry for Boomer," she said. "Imagine how it must feel to fall out of a groove. First you're hitting every ball into the stands. And then suddenly you lose it—your confidence. Your timing. Everything."

"So you think it's all in his head?" I asked her.

"That's what I think," she said.

"Any other ideas?" Derek asked.

"Maybe he's sick," Fernando suggested. "Or maybe he's homesick—for Blizzard Creek."

At the mention of Boomer's former town, a strange expression came over PJ's face.

"What's the matter, PJ?" I asked.

PJ sighed. "I hate to even say it. It really makes me mad."

"Hey, this sounds juicy," Fernando said with excitement. "Tell us!"

PJ frowned. "It's a nasty rumor going around. Spread by the Rockets' so-called fans. They say Boomer's still loyal to Blizzard Creek. They think he's losing the games on purpose!"

"On purpose?" Derek said with surprise.

"But it just doesn't make sense," PJ said.

"No? Well, it might make *cents*!" I said, jingling some loose change in my pocket for effect. "Maybe someone in Blizzard Creek is paying him to do it."

"Why would Boomer need any more money?" Fernando asked. "Doesn't he already have a multi-million dollar contract?"

"I'll give you five good reasons," I said. "G-R-E-E-D."

"Boomer's not greedy," PJ said.

15

"And I think it's a little early to start accusing him of selling out," Derek said. "But let's keep it in mind. I say we see what ALEC the computer has to say about slumps."

ALEC is our very intelligent and talkative computer—like Albert Einstein and Speedy Gonzalez combined. Derek tapped on ALEC's keyboard to fire him up.

"Helllooooo, Crew!" ALEC said, moments later.

"Hi, ALEC," Derek said. "Can you help us with a little baseball question? We . . ."

Before Derek could finish his sentence, ALEC was eagerly chatting away. It's a problem he has. His CPU is so stuffed with information that, given the chance, he gushes like Niagara Falls. "Oh, baseball!" he said, cranking up some baseball organ music from his sound system. "America's national pastime! How I love the smell of the fresh-cut grass, the sound of the bat cracking against the ball, the taste of hot-dogs and peanuts, and the fascinating science that makes it all possible."

None of us had the heart to remind ALEC that he couldn't actually smell or taste.

"Science? In baseball?" Fernando asked. "Oh, you mean like the math behind all those goofy statistics?"

"Not at all, Fernando," ALEC said. "The curve of the curve ball, the arc of a deep drive to the outfield . . . it's all pure physics! Not to mention the . . ."

"Hold up, ALEC" Derek said. "How about the science of slumps?"

"Excuse me?" ALEC said.

"We need to know what causes a great hitter to fall into a slump," Derek said.

"Oh! Why didn't you say so?" ALEC asked, whizzing through his electronic files. "Let me check! Hmm, says here that poor hitting could be caused by something psychological—like poor concentration. Or something physical—like an illness or allergy. Or a problem with the bat, or the ball, or with the park itself."

"Hey," I said. "Mr. Derosa did say the problem started on a streak of home games, right? Maybe something at the park is different."

"Could be, Super Crew," ALEC said. "Parks have to be carefully designed and constructed to keep the sun out of hitters' eyes and to minimize the effects of the wind."

"Hey, that might be it," I said.

"What's it?" Derek asked.

"Kinetic City stadium is built right on the waterfront. It's really windy there all the time."

"That's correct, Megan," ALEC chimed in. "The winds off the water are the source of Kinetic City's nickname—The Gusty City. The prevailing winds blow right over the stadium at a nearly constant 35 miles per hour!"

"That could mess up anybody's hitting," I said. "Especially somebody who hits the ball as high as Boomer always does."

"Great idea, Megan," PJ said.

"Thank you, thank you," I said as I bowed deeply.

"Except Kinetic City stadium is the same old park it was when Boomer was hitting home runs," she said.

"Oh, yeah," I mumbled.

"And my meteorology database shows no significant increase or shifts in the prevailing winds over Kinetic City," ALEC added.

"Well that's strike one, I guess" Fernando said.

"Maybe it's not the wind but the weather," Derek said. "It's been pretty cold lately. Couldn't that mess him up?"

"Sure could, Derek," ALEC said. "Your human muscles often tighten up when the temperature drops."

"Wouldn't that affect all the players, though?" PJ said. "Even on the other team?"

"Good point, PJ," ALEC said.

"I still say it's all in his head," PJ said. "He could have pulled out of this slump a long time ago if all the fans weren't such whiny boneheads. He just needs to hear that we're behind him a hundred percent and then he'll be as good as new."

"I just have one more question for ALEC," I said. "Have you ever heard of players being bought off to lose their games?"

PJ looked at me like I was some kind of traitor. Then ALEC emitted a loud DING. "It's sad but true, Megan. In 1919, the Chicago White Sox team was dubbed 'The Black Sox' when nine of its players accepted money in exchange for losing the World Series."

"I can't believe an athlete would do a thing like that," PJ said. "I'm sure Boomer wouldn't, anyway."

I wasn't so sure. I could imagine just about anybody doing something like that if the price was right.

"Well, now we've got confidence problems, illness, homesickness, park problems, bat problems, ball problems, a cold snap, and the ol' 'bought off by the former team' theory," Derek said.

"Right," I said.

"Sounds like we need more information," Fernando said.

"I say we head down to the stadium and start talking to some of these Rockets people," Derek suggested. "Any idea when they play their next game?"

"They're playing . . . right now," PJ said looking at her watch. "The game just started."

"Perfect," Derek said. "ALEC, set course for the Kinetic City stadium."

"You got it," ALEC said, firing up the train's engines. "Oh—and Crew, I've found something here that might interest you."

"What's that?" I asked.

"Guess which team will get to go to the playoffs next month if the KC Rockets don't?" ALEC asked.

"Don't tell them, ALEC," PJ said. "It'll just make them more suspicious."

But ALEC wouldn't be stopped. "The Blizzard Creek Hailstones!" he said.

"It doesn't mean a thing," PJ insisted.

"I don't know, PJ," I said. "I'm not ruling out anything yet. Even cheating." I looked at Derek and Fernando. I could tell they thought the same thing I did. Maybe there was more to this case than just bad hitting. With that on our minds, we made tracks for Kinetic City stadium.

CHAPTER TWO

A Day at the Park

The KC Express zipped us across town to the waterfront, where the KC stadium perched on a peninsula that jutted out into the bay. We parked the train on a side track and hoofed it the rest of the way to the ball park. We were just coming up to the back of the stadium when a huge white limousine came roaring up from behind us. We would have been road-kill if we hadn't jumped out of the way! The limo screeched to a halt by a back gate entrance and a driver dressed in a white uniform jumped out. He ran around to the back door and swung it open. Out stepped a majorly made-up woman, also dressed in white with dark sunglasses and a leather briefcase in her hand. She bolted toward the stadium, and *was about to head inside, but PJ stormed over to give the woman a piece of her mind . . .*

"Excuse me!" PJ shouted. The woman didn't even turn around. "Didn't you see us back there?" PJ started to walk faster to catch up, but the driver stuck out his arm and stopped PJ in her tracks.

"Hold on there, Chickie," the guy said.

"Hey!" PJ said, surprised.

"Ms. Frost is late for an appointment," the driver said. "She don't need no kidlings yapping at her right now."

"But you almost ran over us!" PJ said.

"Why don't you go tell your mommy," the guy said.

By now, Derek, Fernando, and I had walked up, so I chimed in. "Okay, mister, we'll tell somebody. Like the police!" I pulled my case notebook out of my pocket to write down the license plate number. But there weren't any numbers on the plate, just a single word. "FROST?" I said. "Huh. That'll be easy to remember."

"What does 'FROST' mean?" Derek asked.

"That's who owns this car," the driver explained. "My boss, Sally Frost."

I saw PJ's eyes widen and her frown turn into a gasp. "You mean Sally Frost, super agent to the stars?"

The driver turned to PJ. "You've heard of her?"

"Who hasn't?" PJ exclaimed.

"I haven't," Fernando said.

"Not me," Derek said.

"Me either," I shrugged.

"You guys, she's the most powerful agent in sports!" PJ explained. "Name a big-time athlete and she's behind them. Even Boomer Baxter!"

"That's right," the driver said. "Ms. Frost negotiated almost every over-inflated salary in sports. Cool, huh?"

"Great," Derek mumbled.

"I can't believe I was that close to meeting Sally Frost!" PJ said.

"I can't believe I was that close to being killed by Sally Frost," Fernando said.

"Hey, listen," the driver said, "I'm sorry about that, really. It's just that Ms. Frost don't like to be late. Let me make it up to you, huh? How'd you kids like a ride around the parking lot in the limo? I bet you've never ridden in nothing this big!"

Boy, was he wrong about that! The KC Express could carry about twenty limos with room to spare.

"Mister, you have no idea," Derek said.

"Huh?" the driver replied.

"Never mind," I laughed. "Come on, Crew. Let's go."

As we walked around the side of the stadium, PJ pointed out all the stuff the stadium owners had done to spruce it up now that the Rockets were finally selling some tickets. Kinetic City stadium used to be a shabby, low-key kind of place. But now the parking lot had been repaved, the entrance gates had been painted Rockets Red, and the crumbling brick walls of the stadium had been repaired and cleaned. There was even a giant flower bed out front with flowers of all different colors growing in the shape of a rocket lifting off from the launch pad.

"Isn't this place the greatest?" PJ exclaimed.

"Yeah, but it looks like they're not finished," Fernando said. He pointed to a huge blue tarp hanging on the outside of the stadium. It was about thirty feet wide and it reached from the top of the stadium wall all the way to the ground. As it flapped in the gusting wind, we could see some sort of metal scaffold underneath. A gray-haired man in a blue suit was standing in front of the tarp handing out flyers to people as they walked by. As we got closer he smiled at us and held out a handful for us to take.

"Hey there, kids. How are you today?"

"Fine," we all said.

"I'm Al Charboni, owner and founder of the Grand Slam Grill."

"Cool!" Fernando exclaimed. "That's my favorite place!"

"Me, too!" I said.

"That's what I like to hear!" Mr. Charboni

beamed. "Did you kids know I came to this country thirty years ago with nothing but the clothes on my back, a pound of hamburger in my pocket, and a deep fat fryer? From that I have built the twenty-eighth largest fast-food chain in the tri-state area."

We all 'ooh'ed' and 'ahh'ed.' Well, except for Derek.

"You kids will definitely want to enter my drawing," Mr. Charboni said.

"What do you mean?" I asked.

"It's all right there on the flyer," Mr. Charboni said.

Derek read out loud, *"The Grand Slam Grill Grand Unveiling Contest! Join the Grand Slam Grill in celebrating the greatest season in Rockets' history. Make plans to attend the season finale double-header between the Rockets and the Blue Sox, when we will unveil the amazing new Grand Slam Grill sign in a special ceremony."*

"New sign?" Fernando asked.

"Yes sir!" Mr. Charboni said. "It's right

here behind this tarp." He patted the scaffolding with pride. "When the time comes, we throw the switch and this baby will rise up on this platform I had built and lock into place. Then people all over the world will know about the Grand Slam Grill!"

"What was wrong with the old sign?" Fernando asked. "I loved that bullseye!"

"Bullseye?" Derek asked.

"Well, actually, it was a giant tomato slice," PJ said. "If a batter hit it, everybody in the stadium won a free order of fries."

"It was awesome!" Fernando said.

"It was an eyesore," Mr. Charboni said. "That old sign was up there for twenty years. It was peeling and faded. So now, with the Rockets on TV so much, I had it taken down. Then I decided to go all out and have a fancy new sign made to introduce my latest, greatest menu item just in time for the World Series!"

"Wow, what is it?" Fernando asked. "A quadruple burger? Chili nachos? Sausage on a stick?"

"Oh, that's a secret, my boy," Mr. Charboni smiled. "You'll have to come to the last game and find out when we raise the sign into its spot. But I guarantee it will make your mouth water and your heart skip a beat!"

"With all that grease, I'm sure it will skip a beat," Derek whispered to me.

"So what's the contest part?" PJ asked.

"Keep reading," Mr. Charboni said.

Derek looked down at the flyer. *"You can be a part of the Grand Slam Grill's history! Just fill out the form below and drop it in the box at our KC stadium location. We'll draw one name during the break between games. That lucky person will get to come down on the field and hit the switch that will raise the new sign into place! Then they'll go home with $1,000 in Grand Slam Grill gift certificates. It could be you!"*

"That's great!" Fernando said.

"Oh, yeah, a real historic milestone," Derek said sarcastically.

"Be sure to fill out your entry forms, kids!" Mr. Charboni said.

We promised we would—well, except for Derek—and we hurried into the stadium.

Once we were inside, I saw why Mr. Charboni had his old sign taken down. All the other advertisers in town had really gone crazy when the team's season got off the ground. They'd put up all new banners that flapped in the ocean breeze, repainted old billboards, and put up new advertisements on the scoreboard. The place looked great. But unfortunately, the atmosphere in the stadium was anything but festive and the scoreboard showed us why: the Rockets were down 4-0 already.

"This stinks," PJ said, as we scooted into some seats right above the Rockets' dugout. "The Rockets don't deserve this!"

"You can say that again," I said. "These advertisers should have put their money behind a team that can win!"

"Megan, I didn't mean *that*," PJ said.

We turned our attention to the field, but even with our decent seats, it was hard to see. Baseball fever had inspired a lot of the fans to wear caps with two-foot-tall foam rockets perched on top. Whenever anyone moved, the rocket hats rocked back and forth. It kind of made me seasick. "Excuse me," I said to two college-age guys in front of us. "You're blocking our view."

One of them turned around. "Lucky you," he said. "This team is painful to watch anyway."

He was right. For the next few innings, there wasn't much to see. Even when Boomer came up to bat, nothing much happened to give us any clues to his slump. He was walked once and struck out once. Somewhere in the seventh inning Derek fell asleep, but a gust of wind blew a hot dog wrapper right in his face and scared him awake. He jumped about ten feet in the air, but then he tried to look like nothing happened. Being cool must be so much work.

But then in the eighth inning the Rockets managed to score two runs to make it 4-2. They held the visiting team scoreless in the top of the ninth, and as the Rockets came up to bat, the crowd started to get energized a bit.

"Come on, Rockets, you can do it!" PJ yelled, standing on her seat and peering over the hats in front of her.

The first batter for the Rockets came up to home plate. I thought he looked pretty relaxed, but PJ could tell by his posture that he'd already given up. And she was right. He struck out in three swings. Then the second batter popped out on the first pitch. Suddenly it was two outs with no one on. People started to file out of the stadium.

But then the next player was walked, and the fourth batter managed to knock a line drive down the third-base line.

"A base hit!" Fernando exclaimed.

"Two men on!" PJ said. "Maybe the Rockets can do it!"

The crowd was getting more revved up now. The two guys in front of us started cheering and leaping up and down so fast it looked like the foam rockets on their heads had springs. But their cheers turned to boos when the next batter came up to hit. It was Boomer Baxter!

"Uh oh. Pressure's on," PJ said. "If he hits a homer, they'll win . . . AND they'll go to the playoffs!"

"But if he gets out, that's the game," Fernando said.

Boomer swung on the first ball and got a strike.

"A lefty should have a good chance against this pitcher," PJ said.

But when the second pitch came up, Boomer swung and missed again. Strike two!

The crowd erupted in frustration. "That guy can't hit anything!" someone yelled. "Send him back to Blizzard Creek!"

"Come on, Boomer," PJ said. "Hit it like you used to. Knock it over the fence!"

The third pitch came in fast, but it was over the plate and this time Boomer was right on it. The bat struck the ball with a hard crack. The crowd fell silent as it watched the ball soar. All the players' heads turned toward right field as the ball shot through the sky. We all rose to our feet to see as it went up . . . up . . . up . . .

Maybe he'd done it!

CHAPTER THREE

Angles in the Outfield

With two men on base, and his team down by two runs, Boomer Baxter hit a high fly ball out to right field. For a moment, everyone in the stadium held their breath as the ball flew toward the outfield wall . . .

"Go, Boomer!" PJ yelled.

"It's all yours, baby!" Fernando added.

"I think he's going to . . ." But before I could finish my sentence, I realized that the ball was dropping down way too fast and too soon.

"Oh no," PJ cried.

With total ease, the guy in right field stuck out his glove and caught the ball. Out! And three outs for the KC Rockets meant the game was over.

"That Baxter loser is the worst thing that's happened to Kinetic City since the flood of 1943," grumbled an old man behind us.

"No he's not!" PJ said to him.

"You're right. He's worse!" said the man's wife. "A flood doesn't have a five-year contract."

Everyone around us got up and began heading out of the stands. If we were going to catch Rudy Derosa and Boomer before they left the stadium, we had to hurry. They were probably already trying to get away from the reporters.

"Come on," I said. "Let's get to the dugout!"

We fought our way through the crowd of unhappy fans. We flashed our Super Crew ID cards to the security guards and they let us onto the field. PJ spotted Rudy Derosa standing next to the dugout. He was a short guy with red side burns, wearing a Rockets cap and jacket and chewing a hunk of bubble gum so hard and fast he looked like an overstressed cow.

"Mr. Derosa?" I said as we approached.

"Super Crew!" he said. "Did you see the game?"

"Unfortunately," I said.

"Now you know why I can't sleep nights anymore." Mr. Derosa said. "Here I am, spittin'-distance away from my first series playoffs, and what happens? My sure-bet home-run hitter's blooping balls into the outfield."

"He didn't look too good," PJ admitted. "But don't worry, we have some ideas about what might be going on."

"Good," said Mr. Derosa. " 'Cause all my ideas involve whacking Boomer on the head!"

"Maybe we should run through our list," Derek said quickly. He pulled out a piece of paper from his pocket. "Let's see. What about this: Do you think maybe Boomer has just psyched himself out? Lost confidence or some-thing?"

Mr. Derosa shrugged, blew a big bubble, and let it pop. "I don't know," he said, going back to his chewing. "At first that's what I thought it was. But, usually a confidence problem translates into a change in motion, ya know? Late timing. Different bat position.

36

Something like that. But we compared old and new films. And I swear you can't see one lick of difference between the way he's hitting now and the way he hit early in the season."

"Really," PJ said. "That's weird."

"So I had a talk with him and told him I believed he'd turn it around. I even promised to keep him in the lineup so he wouldn't lose his touch. But it hasn't worked."

"How about his bat?" Fernando asked. "Did he switch brands or anything?"

Mr. Derosa shook his head. "As far as I know, he's been using the same bat for the last three years."

"Maybe it's worn out," I suggested.

"Not the exact same bat," Mr. Derosa explained to me. "Hitters switch their bats every two or three weeks. But he always uses the same kind of bat. Made to his exact specifications at a factory across the state in Bellfrey County. Once a hitter finds a winning bat, they don't usually like to change anything."

"And no one's switching balls on him, are they?" Derek asked.

"Not a chance," Mr. Derosa said. "That part's highly regulated by the League."

"Do you think maybe he's just cold?" PJ asked.

"Cold?" Mr. Derosa asked. "Heck, I doubt it. He's from Blizzard Creek. Up there, they go swimming in July."

"What's so great about that?" Fernando asked.

"The lakes don't melt till August!" Mr. Derosa said.

"Oh," Derek said, peering at his list. "Well, let's see. We have two other ideas. First, has anything changed here in the ballpark that could make it hard for him to hit?"

"Are you kidding?" Mr. Derosa said. "This is one of the oldest parks in the U.S. of A. They haven't changed anything but the prices in about fifty years."

"Sure they have," PJ said. "They've added lights. They've put up new signs. They've—"

"Yeah, okay you're right," Mr. Derosa said. "They've made a lot of—what do they call it—

cosmetic changes to the ballpark. I hate all that fancy stuff. But it's all window dressing. I don't think it's making Boomer mess up."

"But the lights could be in his eyes," Fernando said. "Or maybe all those new signs are distracting him."

"With some other player, I'd say maybe," Mr. Derosa said. "But not with Boomer. He's Mr. Zen Master, if you know what I mean."

"I don't," Derek said.

"Oh, you know, he's into all that meditation and deep breathing mumbo jumbo," Mr. Derosa said, rolling his eyes. "He's always reading some book or another about that kind of stuff."

"Really?" Derek asked, surprised.

"Yup. Boomer could stay focused even if the pitcher was throwing grenades."

"So, then, what about this rumor?" Fernando said, lowering his voice. "Do you think he might really be throwing his game?"

For the first time, Mr. Derosa didn't immediately shake his head. He blew another bubble till it popped. "I'm beginning to wonder, actually," he said finally. "I've always thought there was something a little weird about Boomer."

"Weird?" PJ asked. "What do you mean?"

"Well, there's all that meditation stuff I mentioned, but on top of that the guy doesn't eat hot dogs," Mr. Derosa said. "He doesn't drink soda pop."

"No way. Then what does he eat?" Fernando asked.

Mr. Derosa grimaced. "It's all this health food stuff. Tofu. Seaweed. Vegetables. Isn't that weird?"

"Wait a second," Derek said with a laugh. "Just because he likes health food doesn't mean he's weird."

"I don't know," Mr. Derosa said. "I have trouble trusting a guy who doesn't like a good sirloin. As a matter of fact, I thought that might be just what was wrong with him. All that froufy food's making him weak. Told him I'd spring for a couple of cheeseburgers at the Grand Slam Grill if it would give him some more energy. But he said no thanks. See what I mean? What kind of person wouldn't accept free burgers?"

PJ was about to jump to Boomer's defense, but she was interrupted by a Rockets player who'd overheard our conversation.

"Rudy's right. Boomer isn't like the rest of us," the player confirmed. "Every week we invite him to come bowling with us, but he always has some goofy reason for not going. What was it last week, Rudy?"

"He had to empty his compost bin," the manager sighed.

"And get this," another player piped in, "the guy's the highest paid player on the team. He has enough money for a really hot sports car, but instead he rides a bike everywhere!"

Mr. Derosa nodded. "Funny guy. Real funny guy."

"You guys are all wrong about Boomer. He's the best!" PJ said. "Just because he rides a bike doesn't make him a cheater!"

"No, but it all adds up to a guy who's not really a team player," one of the Rockets replied. "It makes it easy to believe the guy's not too loyal, if you know what I mean."

"Maybe we'd better go talk to Boomer ourselves," I suggested. "Where can we find him?"

"He'll be back there in the locker room, doing his yoga," Mr. Derosa told us. "But you kids aren't allowed in there. Stay put. I'll go tell him to come talk to you. But listen, whatever you can do, do it quick. Tomorrow's the last day of the season. We've got a double-header with the Blue Sox, and we have to win one of those games or it's all over but the firing, if you know what I mean." Then the manager turned and headed for the locker room.

"Can you believe those jocks?" Derek said with disgust. "They're like sheep! Everyone has to act the same, eat the same, and buy the same stuff . . . or else they're weird."

"Sounds like junior high to me," PJ said.

We sat and waited for what we thought would be just a couple of minutes. But five minutes turned to ten, which turned to fifteen and twenty. Soon all of us were getting restless.

I stood up and walked to the far end of the dugout. In the corner I saw the microphone they used for the National Anthem. "Do you think this thing is still on?" I asked. I pulled it out of its stand and flipped on the switch. "Testing, one, two, three," I said, as my voice reverberated through the stands.

"Megan, you're going to get us in trouble," Derek said.

"Nah, we're the Super Crew, remember?" I said. "We just have to say we're on official business."

"You're mad with power," Derek joked.

"That's me," I said. "I think I'll practice for when I win that Grand Slam Grill drawing." I took a deep breath and belted out my best rendition of the Grand Slam Grill jingle.

"Take me out for a burger!
Take me out for some fries!
Buy me a shake and a chili dog,
I don't care if my arteries clog!
Oh, it's root, root, root beer and ice cream
We'll scarf till we've had our fill!

For it's one, two, three meals a day
At the Grand Slam Grill!"

Then, my so-called friends all grabbed their ears and screamed in horror.

"Oh, the agony!" Derek cried.

"My ears!" PJ yelled.

"Run, before she kills again!" Fernando laughed. The three of them took off toward left field. Fernando grabbed my Rockets cap off my head as he went by.

"Hey, give it back!" I yelled as I chased them across the field. Just as I reached Fernando, he whipped my cap over to PJ like a frisbee.

"Think fast, PJ!" he said. But she wasn't paying attention. Something had caught her eye back at the dugout. The cap bounced off her shoulder and I snatched it up.

"Look, it's Boomer!" PJ said pointing.

She was right. Boomer and another person were deep in conversation in the dugout.

"Who is that with him?" Fernando asked.

"Probably a reporter," Derek said.

"I don't think so," PJ said. She squinted. "That person's wearing all white. I think it's Sally Frost!"

"Really?" I said.

"I'm positive," PJ said. "C'mon. Let's go."

But just as we started back across the field, we heard a strange gurgling noise coming up from the grass.

"What is *that*?" Fernando asked nervously.

We didn't have to wait for an answer. Suddenly, powerful jets of cold water started shooting out of the ground from every direction. It was like being caught in the middle of an instant monsoon. Somebody had turned on the sprinkler system!

CHAPTER FOUR

Field of Streams

As soon as the sprinkler jets blasted on, we all screamed from the surprise and the cold and took off running in different directions like the four blind mice. None of us could see a thing. The wind kept blowing the water right in our eyes. Anybody watching us run around the outfield in soggy circles would have died laughing, I'm sure. By the time we got our bearings and made a dash for the dugout, Boomer was gone and we were all completely soaked. Sally Frost was still there, packing up her briefcase. She didn't look too thrilled to meet us . . .

"Excuse me!" Sally Frost said with a scowl. "I don't know who you people are, but you don't belong here and you're getting my documents wet!"

"Sorry about that, Ms. Frost," PJ said, water dripping off the end of her nose.

"How do you know my name?" the agent snapped. "Who are you?"

"We're the Kinetic City Super Crew," I said.

"Is that supposed to mean something to me?" Ms. Frost replied.

"Do you know where Boomer went?" Fernando asked.

"I sent him home. Why do you ask?"

"We're here to help Boomer get out of his slump," PJ explained.

Sally Frost gave us a look of disbelief. "And how does skipping through the sprinkler system help Mr. Baxter, I wonder?" she said. Oof. This woman was rough.

"Mr. Derosa told us to wait out here for Boomer," I said. "Then we kinda got caught in the crossfire."

"I see," Ms. Frost replied. "Well, I don't approve of this one bit. Derosa never consulted me about calling in outside help, and frankly I don't see how a bunch of children could do anything but harm to my client."

"But . . ." I started.

"No! I mean it," Ms. Frost interrupted. "This is highly irregular. Boomer does nothing without my approval. All business transactions go through me, do you understand?"

"But we don't get paid to help . . ." Derek tried to explain.

"I don't care. You drippy slackers keep away from my client. He's under enough stress as it is! This whole lousy town is after Boomer like wolves on a lame sheep." She snapped her briefcase shut and turned to leave. "Now if you'll excuse me, I need to get back to Blizzard Creek before dark."

"Blizzard Creek?" I exclaimed.

Sally Frost turned and said, "Yes, Blizzard Creek. That's where I work. Do you have a problem with that?"

"No, no," I stammered. "I just, you know . . . I've never met anyone from there. It's cold there, I hear."

Ms. Frost gave me a strange look. "Yes. It is. Very cold." Then she turned and headed for the exit.

"That was one of the most paranoid people I've ever met," Derek said matter-of-factly.

"I can't believe she told us to stay away from Boomer," PJ said.

"I wouldn't worry about her," Fernando said.

"You guys! Don't you see?" I said.

"What?" the Crew responded.

Sometimes they could be so dense. "Sally Frost is the payoff connection!"

"What are you talking about, Megan?" Derek asked.

"Didn't you hear her? She said 'all business transactions go through me.' Boomer doesn't do anything unless she says so. *She's from Blizzard Creek*. I'm telling you, she's the middle man, er, woman for the whole deal. And she wants us to stay away from Boomer because she's afraid we'll find her out!"

"I take it back. *You* are the most paranoid person I've ever met," Derek said.

"Boomer is not cheating!" PJ said.

"We'll see," I said. "We'll see."

Fernando found a box of towels under the bench and we tried to dry off, but our clothes were so soaked, it was pretty useless. We were freezing and Boomer was long gone, so we decided to head back to the KC Express.

"Hey! Who's that in the dugout?" a voice called out from the field. We all looked up and saw a group of reporters heading for us. As soon as they recognized us, they got very excited.

"If the Super Crew's here, Derosa must be really worried!" one of them commented.

When the first reporter reached us, she started right in with the questions. "Super Crew," she said. "Have you been called in to find out what's wrong with Boomer Baxter?"

"No comment," Derek said quickly.

"That means yes!" said the reporter.

"Is it true what we've heard? Is Boomer throwing the games?" asked another reporter.

"That could be one area of our investigation," I said, thinking I was being quite subtle. But it wasn't good enough for Derek.

"Megan," he said. "Don't say anything to them."

"You gettin' this, Millie?" one of the reporters said to another.

"Every word," Millie responded.

"We need to get out of here," PJ said. "C'mon." She pushed through the crowd of reporters and ran off toward the parking lot. We followed right behind her. And the reporters followed right behind us.

"No comment, no comment, no comment, no comment," Derek yelled over his shoulder as the reporters continued to pelt us with questions. Finally we made it to the KC Express Train. We leapt aboard and closed the door.

"Phew!" Fernando said. "I say we go to Boomer's house right away and get his side of the story."

"Good idea," Derek said. "This is out of control."

"Stupid reporters," PJ said crossly. "They're the ones causing this whole mess."

She leaned out the train window and yelled down to the reporters, "Remember, you guys . . ." She glanced at me, too, when she said it, "Boomer's innocent until proven guilty!"

CHAPTER FIVE

Get a Clue

Leaving the nosy reporters in our wake, we headed off to Boomer's house on the other side of Kinetic City. It was obvious that the rest of the Crew wasn't ready to buy into the rumors about Boomer cheating, so on the trip across town I decided to find out a little more about his agent, Sally Frost. I turned to our number-one snooping—I mean research—aid, ALEC the computer . . .

"Well, Megan," ALEC said. "My databases tell me that Sally Frost was born and raised in Blizzard Creek. She attended Our Lady of Frostbite High School, she graduated from Glacier College with a degree in sports marketing, and she started the Frost Sports Talent Agency ten years ago."

"Hmm," I said. "That doesn't tell me much, ALEC. "Can you give me some more details?"

"That question is music to my audio receptors!" ALEC beeped. His wall-sized monitor pulsed with color and then he continued. "What else would you like to know? I have her shoe size, her mother's maiden name, the phone number of her plumber, satellite photos of her dog, a list of all her video rentals for the last three years . . ."

"ALEC, stop!" I said. "That's not the kind of information I need."

"Oh, sorry," our computer replied.

"I was thinking more along the lines of what she did before she started her sports agency," I said.

"Ohhh," ALEC said. "Heck, that's easy. She worked in the front office of the Blizzard Creek Hailstones baseball team."

"Ah ha!" I yelled. "I knew it! I knew there was a connection between that woman and Boomer's old team. This gets fishier by the minute." I decided to wait until after we talked to Boomer to tell the rest of the Crew what I had learned. I couldn't wait to get his side of the story.

When we arrived at Boomer's house, we walked up the short sidewalk and I reached for the door bell. Derek stopped me, though. Then he stepped back and frowned as he looked at the house.

"Are you sure this is the right place?" he asked.

"Sure," I said. "I got the address from ALEC. Why?"

"Well, it's just that this house is so . . . I don't know . . ."

"Boring," Fernando said.

"That's not exactly what I was thinking," Derek said, "but it is pretty plain. I expected a huge mansion. Something that showed off Boomer's millions."

"I told you guys he's not like that," PJ said. "He's not a showoff. He's . . ."

"Boring," Fernando said.

"Fernando!" PJ yelled.

Suddenly the front door opened just a

crack and a deep but soft voice said, "Can you keep it down? I'm trying to read."

"Boomer? Boomer Baxter?" I said.

"No, sorry, wrong house. This is the, uh, Kant residence."

"Kant?" Derek said. "You mean like Emmanuel Kant, the eighteenth-century philosopher?"

The door swung wide open and there stood Boomer Baxter. "Yeah! Exactly! How did you know that?" Boomer said.

"Oh, Derek knows lots of things that will never make him any money," I said.

"Could somebody tell me what's going on?" Fernando said. "Why is Boomer staying at some dead philosopher's house?"

Derek laughed. "Don't worry about it, Nando."

"Are you guys the Super Crew?" Boomer asked.

"That's us," PJ said. Her eyes were glittering and she was flashing a really cheesy smile. She was totally starstruck.

"Sorry about lying to you like that," Boomer said. "I've just had so many people knocking on my door to yell at me. It's really out of hand. Come on in."

We stepped into Boomer's house and he led us to the living room. The inside of Boomer's house was just as plain as the outside: white walls, wood floors, basic furniture. There were a lot of book shelves, though, and a framed Masters Degree diploma hung over a reading desk.

"Check it out," Derek said, pointing at the walls of books. "I had this guy all wrong."

Boomer plopped down into a chair and sighed. He was a big guy with beefy arm muscles. But he didn't look tough, really. He was wearing a T-shirt with a picture of a whale on it that said 'Save Our Seas,' old jeans, and sandals.

"Sorry to bug you at home," I said. "But you were supposed to come talk to us when you got out of the locker room."

"Sure, Rudy mentioned that," Boomer said, scratching nervously on his shoulder. "But I had a meeting. And then I had to get home for an important phone call."

"Sure you did," I said.

Derek jabbed me in the arm with his elbow.

"Well, it's also true I didn't feel like talking to you kids," Boomer admitted.

I poked Derek right back.

"Why not?" PJ asked.

"I'm just tired of talking to people about my slump," he explained. "That's all anyone ever talks to me about. Slump, slump, slump. Why doesn't anyone ask me what I think about world hunger? Who I'm voting for for president? How I plan to save the Kinetic River?"

"Maybe because you're being paid to hit, not to think," Fernando said.

Boomer put his hands on his head. "Don't remind me," he moaned.

"*That* was helpful," Derek said to Fernando.

"We really think we can help you, Boomer," PJ insisted.

"Don't bother," Boomer said. "I've figured it out. I think all I need is a new perspective. A slump's only a problem if you see it as a problem. Do you get my drift?"

Personally, I had no idea what he was talking about. But Derek nodded his head right away.

"Sure," Derek said. "You mean, if you look at it differently, maybe it's not a bad thing at all. Maybe it can teach you something about yourself."

"Exactly," Boomer said, smiling for the first time since we'd arrived.

"That's beautiful," I said. "But while you're busy learning stuff, your slump is going to be the ruin of your manager, your team, and this whole town."

Boomer's smile disappeared at once. "Good point."

"So, Boomer," PJ said, getting back to business. "Are you totally psyched out now? Like there's no way you could hit another homer?"

"Not really," he said. "I meditate before every game. And when I'm up at bat, I feel just as focused and confident as I used to. Like I could hit the ball to China!"

"So you *do* meditate, huh?" Derek asked, looking more impressed every moment.

Boomer nodded. "I get most of my ideas from Benjazi Ripken, Jr., the Zen guru of baseball." He plucked a book from the shelf and handed it to Derek. "This is my favorite: 'The Sound of One Bat Swinging.' "

While Derek flipped through the book, Boomer paused and took a few sniffs of the air. "Hang on. I think my dinner's ready. You kids don't mind if I start eating, do you?"

" 'Course not," Fernando said as he sniffed too. "Smells good!"

"I'd be happy to share," Boomer said. "I made a big tofu and beet casserole."

"Oh. We, uh, just ate. And I'm allergic to beets," Fernando said quickly. He looked a little green. "They make me swell up. It's gross. Really."

Boomer got up and went to the kitchen. While he clinked around with his dishes, Fernando whispered, "Tofu and beet casserole! Rudy Derosa was right—this guy is loopy!"

"Fernando, that's so mean," PJ said.

Boomer came back with a plate full of food. He sat down and began eating it up. "The rest of the team is having dinner out at Tommy's House of Sausage," he said. "Can you imagine?"

"Yes, I can," Fernando said. "Why don't we go join them?"

"No way," Boomer said, stuffing a big chunk of tofu into his mouth. "That stuff is pure poison. Last time I ate a sausage I had pork burps for a week! Besides, I think hogs are meant to be hogs; not pork. I think cows are meant to be cows; not beef. I'm a vegetarian now—through and through."

"That makes sense," Derek said.

"Yeah, but it bums out the rest of the team," Boomer said. "They think I'm not a team player because I won't eat where they eat."

"You do like being on the team, don't you?" I asked.

"It's okay, I guess," Boomer said with a shrug. "I mean, if you're going to be an over-paid professional athlete, then this is probably the place to do it. It's just . . . well, I was happier before I was a star."

"You were?" I asked with disbelief.

"Sure," Boomer said. "I don't like all the attention. The photos. The promotions. The talk shows. As soon as I retire, I'm going to live in a hut and write and paint."

Whoa. Boomer didn't like being a star hitter? Maybe he had another reason for playing bad baseball—like getting out of his contract, or getting rid of the fans' attention.

I was becoming more convinced of Boomer's guilt. But Derek looked like he was becoming more convinced he was a decent guy.

"Hey, Boomer," he said, "do you think maybe your bats could be causing your slump?"

"My bats?" Boomer asked. "Not a chance. They're the best money can buy, made just the way I want them. And I just got a new batch from the factory two weeks ago."

"Two weeks ago?" PJ asked. "Isn't that when your slump started?"

Boomer stopped mid-chew to think. "As a matter of fact, it was."

"That can't be a coincidence," Derek said.

"Maybe they sent you the wrong bats," PJ said.

"No," Boomer said. "When they make my bat, they put my name right on the side! See?"

he said. He reached behind his chair and pulled out a bat for us to see.

"Cool," I said. "That's better than a monogrammed wallet."

"Maybe somebody switched your bats on purpose," Fernando suggested.

"Why would anyone want to do that?" Boomer asked.

"Could we see an old bat?" Derek asked. "To compare the two?"

Boomer shook his head. "As soon as I wear out a bat, I recycle it. By now, all my old bats are probably park benches and baby blocks. But if you want to make sure this is mine, just make sure it's the same size and weight as the bats Babe Ruth used. That's the bat I use, too. They have all the details on Ruth's bat over at the Hueyville Slugger Bat Company. That's where I get these made." He handed his bat over to Derek.

Just then, the telephone rang.

"Oops," Boomer said, reaching for the cordless phone in front of him. "That's probably the call I've been waiting for. Could you give me a couple of minutes?"

We nodded. He answered the phone and took it into the kitchen.

"Isn't he the greatest?" PJ gushed.

"He's not at all what I pictured," Derek replied. "I like him."

"Yeah, he's pretty cool," Fernando said. "For a tofu eater."

I stood up and pointed down the hall. "I'll be right back. I'm going to see if Boomer will let me have a bite of that casserole." It wasn't true. But I figured I'd leave those guys to form their own Boomer fan club while I did some real investigating. In other words, I wanted to know who that 'important' phone call was from. Could it be from someone in Blizzard Creek? I had to find out.

I headed into the hall and paused outside the kitchen. Boomer was leaning against the refrigerator, deep in conversation.

"You're sure you still want to go through with this?" he asked. There was a pause as he listened to the person on the other end of the line. "No, no," he said then. His voice sounded tired.

"I'm not backing out now. I made a promise."

Backing out of what? I held my breath and listened for more.

"Sure I'm feeling lousy," Boomer said. "This goes against everything I believe in."

Everything he believed in? He was doing something seriously bad.

Boomer paused again as the caller's voice crackled through on the line. "Well, don't worry about me," he said. "At least it'll all be over tomorrow night. Good. Right. Right. Okay. See you then."

He hung up the phone and let out a long sigh.

I couldn't believe my ears. Talk about suspicious! I had to tell the rest of the Crew—this was our biggest clue yet!

I hurried back into the living room, all set to stun the rest of the Crew with my news. But instead they stunned me.

"Megan," PJ said with dismay. "Look what we found in Boomer's baseball philosophy book." She handed me a piece of paper. At the top it said: 'From The Desk of Sally Frost.'

"Read it," Fernando said.

I scanned the handwritten page.

Boomer,

I know you're torn about going through with this plan, but sometimes you have to do things you don't like to get what you want. In the end I think you'll see that the risk of a little humiliation now will end up being a great moment for you in the end. And don't worry about dealing with the money. I'll take care of everything, just like always.

Bye from Blizzard Creek,

Sally

p.s.—If you need any help making it look natural, I would be glad to give you some pointers. After all, I've helped a lot of other clients pull this off, too.

I was speechless! But Derek read the look on my face. "That letter could be about anything, Megan," he said. "It doesn't mean Boomer's cheating."

"Oh, yeah?" I said. "Well I think you caught PJ's star-struck disease and you can't admit that this guy is looking guiltier by the minute. Wait till I tell you what I just heard."

But just then, Boomer came into the room. I quickly stuffed the note in my pocket. "Sorry to keep you waiting, Super Crew," he said.

"That's okay," I said. "It gave us time to think of some more questions to ask you."

"That's right," Fernando said. "Like, why aren't you more friendly with the rest of the team?"

"I don't know," Boomer said, looking uncomfortable. "I guess I'm sort of an independent type."

"And why do you still deal with an agent from Blizzard Creek? Don't you consider that a little disloyal to Kinetic City?" I asked.

Boomer frowned. "Sally's been my agent from the beginning. It doesn't matter where she's from. Besides, I have interests in Blizzard Creek that she looks after for me."

"Like what?" Fernando asked.

"That's none of your business," Boomer said.

"You're right, Boomer, it's none of our business," PJ said. "Leave him alone, you two."

"Well, could you tell us exactly what you've been doing with your multimillion-dollar salary?" I asked.

fore Boomer could answer, though, k stood up and spoke. "Okay, Crew. Enough estions. I'm sure Mr. Baxter has many more important things to do with his time."

Boomer nodded at Derek appreciatively.

"Thanks for talking with us," Derek said. "We'll be in touch if we find out anything about your bats."

About the bats? Was Derek still stuck on his goofy 'defective bats' theory?

"Better hurry," Boomer said. "We've only got two more games left in the season."

"See ya, Boomer," I said halfheartedly. "It's been real." Yeah. Like, real revealing. "I think Boomer is definitely caught up in something big," I said as we left the house, "and I want to find out what it is!"

CHAPTER SIX

Bats in Bellfrey

*Back on the train, we had a pretty lively
discussion. I told the crew what I'd heard
Boomer say over the phone, and we read over the
note from Sally Frost again. It was enough to
convince Fernando that Boomer was being paid by
Sally Frost to hit badly. But Derek was not about
to believe anything until we had more solid
evidence. He was right about needing better
proof I guess, but my gut still told me something
weird was going on. Even PJ admitted that what
we found made Boomer look bad . . .*

"He really said, 'This goes against everything I
believe in. But at least it will be over tomorrow
night'?" PJ asked.

I nodded.

"I can't believe it," she said. "He stinks!"

"PJ," I said with surprise. "I never thought you'd say anything bad about a Rockets' player."

"Well," PJ said, "if it's true, he's hurting the whole rest of the team!"

Derek spoke up again. "I think you all are jumping to conclusions. Boomer seemed great to me."

"You just like him because he's not a typical jock," Fernando said.

"No, I just think he seems, well, thoughtful," Derek said. "And smart. I think before we do anything else, we have to find out more about his bats. It's too much of a coincidence that his new shipment and his slump arrived on the same day."

"You're not going to let go of this defective bat thing, are you?" I said.

"It's the only lead we have," Derek said. "Besides, if you're so gung-ho about this cheating angle, then we have to eliminate every other possibility before we go public with it. We can't be wrong about that kind of accusation."

Once again, I had to admit Derek was right. "Okay, when should we go?" I sighed.

"First thing tomorrow morning," Derek said. "Then, if we don't turn up a bat problem, we can spend the whole rest of the day checking out any other leads."

Bright and early the next morning, the train took us to Bellfrey County, where the Hueyville Slugger Bat Company had its headquarters. It was a solid brick, four-story structure that sprawled out over an enormous lot. Small metal windows were evenly spaced across the exterior walls, and many of them were covered with metal bars.

"This place looks like a jail," Fernando observed. "Why do we always end up going to the spookiest looking places?"

I led everyone up the stairs, and then pressed the bell.

"Megan," PJ said. "Why did you do that?"

"Why do you think?" I asked. "To get somebody to let us in."

"But we haven't come up with a reason for being here," PJ said. "If they know we're here

71

to uncover information about their bats, we'll never find out the truth about Boomer's."

Oops. She had a point. But it was too late now. We saw a shadow moving behind the windows, and suddenly the doors opened and a hefty man greeted us. He was wearing a light-blue shirt and a yellow bow tie.

"Yes?" he asked, looking mildly suspicious. "What can I do for you?"

We were only silent for a split second before all of us spoke at once.

"We're here for an interview," said Derek.

"We're here for a tour," said PJ.

"We're here to check for roaches," I said.

"We're here to check for aliens," said Fernando.

"Oh, I see," said the man, even more suspiciously.

"What we mean is," I said hurriedly, "We're here for a tour and an interview, because we're hoping to catch some alien roaches."

"Which may have come in on the last space shuttle," Fernando added.

The man raised his right eyebrow in a look of wary skepticism. "Roaches from another planet?" he asked. "That's a new one. You all look a little young to be exterminators," the man said, looking at PJ suspiciously.

"That's because we're not," Derek said quickly. "We're just looking to find the roaches. Not to kill them. It's a project for our biology class."

"I see," said the man. For a moment I thought he was going to let us in. But then he crossed his arms and looked down at us with a rather stern expression. "That's a very nice story. Now please tell me the real reason you're here or I'll call the guard and have him escort you off the property."

"Okay, Mister," PJ said. "The real reason we're here is to see your bats. Your baseball bats."

"That's the only kind we have," he said. "Why do you want to see them?"

"Because—" PJ began. But I didn't let her finish. I didn't want her to tell the truth. I had a better idea.

"Because we're totally wild about baseball and we play it every day and we really wanted to see how bats are made," I blurted out, trying to sound as innocent as PJ. "That's it. No roaches. No aliens. Just an overwhelming love of America's national pastime."

"You play baseball every day?" the man asked. He looked interested. I couldn't back down now.

"Practically every hour," I said.

"You must be good," he said.

"We're amazing," I said. "Especially him," I said, pointing to Derek.

"And you like real, honest-to-goodness all-American wooden bats?"

"Oh, yeah," I said, "we've tried those Canadian bats, but they stink."

"This is extraordinary!" the man said. "I haven't met a kid in years who really appreciates wooden bats. Everybody wants aluminum these days."

"If somebody gave me an aluminum bat," Fernando said, "I'd tell 'em to recycle it into a pie plate and get me a real bat. A wooden bat!"

"So can't you please let us in and tell us all about baseball bats? It would thrill us beyond belief!"

The big guy was practically crying. "You don't know how long I've waited to hear those words!" he gushed. "It's been years since I gave a tour. But here you are! Come in! Come in!" He clapped his hands together and grinned hugely. It was a little weird, actually.

Fernando shot me a look like we'd just set ourselves up for a really bad time. PJ walked in cheerfully. And Derek shook his head.

"Why did you say I was so good?" he whispered, looking mildly panicked. "You're going to get us in trouble!"

"Relax," I told him. "We're not here to play baseball. Just to learn more about it."

We followed the man down a long corridor. He said his name was Elton Asher and he'd been making baseball bats for 37 years.

"Not by myself, mind you," he said. "I have a lot of help from people and computers."

"Oh, really?" Fernando said, trying to look innocent. "What do the computers do?"

"No fair getting ahead of the tour," Mr. Asher said. He leaned into a small office and plucked four visitor passes from a box. "Put these on," he said. "We have a very tight security system in this place."

"Really?" I asked. "You mean like alarms and armed guards?"

"No, like Barney the security guy. But he's enough! He used to be a professional wrestler."

Fernando, PJ, Derek, and I exchanged glances. This place was strange.

"Now then," said Mr. Asher when we had finished sticking the visitor passes onto our jackets. "Are you ready to get started?"

We nodded.

He flashed that too-happy grin again and led us down the sterile hallways of the factory. There wasn't much to see—just a lot of offices and a lot of closed doors. But when he led us downstairs, we heard the whir and whine of machinery.

"Is that where you make the bats?" PJ asked, nodding in the direction of the noise.

"That's our little manufacturing unit," Mr. Asher said. "We'll go there last. But now—" he paused as he dug into his pockets for a key ring loaded with keys, "—now, I'm going to show you where the fun stuff happens."

He unlocked and opened the doors, and ushered us inside. "This," he said grandly, "this is where you sluggers can show me what you're made of!"

"Huh?" I asked, feeling Derek's eyes on me.

"I want you kids to get a chance to do some hitting!" he said happily. He peered over at Derek. "Especially you, Slugger. There's nothing that pleases me more than discovering a fresh new talent."

Uh oh. Now we were in for it!

CHAPTER SEVEN

Let's Get Physical

We'd really done it now. We'd gone and told Mr. Asher that we were all-star ballplayers. And now he was going to put us to the test. If we didn't live up to our reputation at this point, we'd look even more suspicious than if we'd just told the truth to begin with. But there was no turning back. We followed him into the room and waited in the dark . . .

"Behold!" he said when he switched on the lights.

We were standing in an enormous room with a linoleum floor and painted cinderblock walls. The floor was bright green like a well-kept field. It had large, white tiles made to look like the bases, and brown tiles the color of dirt laid out between the bases. Painted on the walls was a sea of faces—the cheering fans up in the stands.

"This place is the coolest," PJ said.

"I thought you'd like it," said Mr. Asher, smiling proudly. He walked over to a set of lockers near the door and began pulling out baseball gear.

"To understand the making of a perfect baseball bat," he said in the same tone of voice my teachers use at the beginning of a lecture, "you must first understand baseball. The *science* of baseball."

"Ah, the science of baseball," Fernando said. "The curve of a curve ball!" He was just repeating the stuff our computer ALEC told us on the train.

"The arc of a deep drive to the outfield!" I chimed in.

"It's all pure physics!" Fernando said conclusively. "Now can we go to the manufacturing room?"

"Nope," said Mr. Asher, "First tell me just *how* it's all about physics."

Oops. I guess we should have listened to ALEC a little longer. We stood around looking at our shoes for a few seconds. Then Mr. Asher tossed PJ a baseball. "C'mon, Pee-wee, you pitch. And you, big guy (he turned to Derek), why don't you take a few swings for me? This will be so nifty!"

As PJ walked toward the pitcher's mound and Derek walked, very slowly, to the batter's box, Mr. Asher spoke. "When you think of hitting a baseball, you should think of Newton."

"Who did he play for?" Fernando asked.

Derek shot Fernando a "duh" look. "Isaac Newton!" he said. "The scientist. You know, the one who got hit on the head with an apple."

"Oh, yeah . . . the gravity guy," Fernando said.

"Right," continued Mr. Asher. "He taught us all about forces like gravity and how they work. And about how and why objects move, and what happens when they hit other objects."

"Like baseballs and bats?" I asked.

"Exactly. When an object is in motion, it has what's called *momentum*. You can think of momentum as the 'oomph' the object would have."

"Oomph?" PJ asked.

"Sure. Like a baseball moving five miles an hour doesn't have as much 'oomph,' or momentum, as a baseball moving at ninety miles per hour. The more speed, the more momentum."

"So," I said, warming up to the subject, "momentum is a measure of how bad you'd feel if the object hit you on the head."

"Yes!" shouted Mr. Asher as if I'd just said something remotely intelligent. "And how would you feel if a bowling ball hit you at ninety miles an hour?"

"Worse than if the baseball hit me," I answered, worried that all this might be leading to a demonstration.

"Right again," he cried. "The other thing that increases momentum is *mass*. The more massive the moving object is, the more 'oomph' it has. Okay, now let's put all this into practice. I've got three bats here, Slugger." Mr. Asher walked toward Derek with three almost identical-looking bats. "Heavy, medium, and light. Choose your weapon."

"Well," said Derek thoughtfully, "if more mass means more momentum, then let's have the heavy one." Mr. Asher smiled and held out one of the bats.

Even though Derek isn't very athletic, he's older and bigger than the rest of us, and he's pretty strong. But we could see from the start that he was having trouble with the heavy bat. He slowly hefted it onto his shoulder and stepped into the batter's box.

"Okay, Pee-wee," Mr. Asher shouted to PJ. "Lemme see your stuff!"

"Nice and easy there, PJ!" I shouted. I knew if she pitched the way she does on the school team, Derek wouldn't have a chance. Unfortunately, she was pretty caught up in the excitement of the situation. She wound up and fired a blistering fastball. Derek barely got the bat off his shoulder before the pitch whizzed by him and thwacked into the wire mesh backstop behind him.

"Try again, Slugger!" Mr. Asher yelled to Derek, and tossed PJ another baseball.

"PJ!" I cried. I gave her a "what are you *doing*" look, and she nodded to me. She wound up and pitched again, a little slower.

Derek started swinging the big bat almost as soon as the ball left PJ's hand. The bat was so heavy, it looked like he was swinging in slow motion. As he spun around, I could see that his face was scrunched up in concentration, and his eyes were closed.

I put my hands over my eyes, but peeked just in time to see Derek somehow, incredibly, hit the pitch squarely. He looked almost as shocked as I did. But the ball just popped up toward PJ, and she caught it easily.

Fernando jumped up immediately to explain. "Derek was just telling me how weak he was feeling, Mr. Asher. From the trip and all. In fact, we're all kind of not feeling ourselves . . ."

"Nonsense!" Mr. Asher exclaimed. I thought he was going to call us impostors right there, and throw us out. "It's the bat! Pure

Florida ironwood, and over fifty-six ounces. Not even Babe Ruth could hit a home run with that."

Now I was confused. "But you said a heavier bat would have more 'oomph'—you know, momentum. So the ball would go farther."

"True," said Mr. Asher. "If Slugger here could swing that bat as fast as he swings a normal bat, then he'd hit the ball a mile. But no one has arms that strong. Not even Babe Ruth."

"So," I said, "a lighter bat is better, because you can swing it faster?"

"Well, let's find out. Here." He threw one of the bats to me. Me and my big mouth. I flinched as I reached out for it. But when I caught it, I was surprised at how light it was.

"Amazing, huh?" said Mr. Asher. "It's reinforced balsa wood. It weighs less than a pound, but we've strengthened it with fibers so it won't shatter. Go on, step into the batter's box."

Great. Now it was my turn. Derek looked at me gratefully as he dragged the heavy bat away from the plate, and I stepped into the batter's box. I looked out at PJ with my "don't make me look like a jerk" look (you kind of have to see it . . .). She nodded, wound up, and delivered a fat pitch right over the plate.

I swung the bat as hard as I could—and missed by a mile. "Try again!" cried Mr. Asher. "That bat's probably a lot lighter than the one you normally use. You have to get used to it."

PJ threw me another easy one. I swung again, and connected with a WHACK. But the bat nearly fell out of my hands, which made me look like a dork. And, even worse, I just slapped the ball right back to PJ. And, just like with Derek's pop up, she caught it easily.

"Hey, what gives?" I was ticked off. It was probably the hardest I'll ever hit a ball, and all I got was a pathetic pop-up.

Mr. Asher chuckled. "That was a decent swing, but that bat just doesn't have much mass. So no matter how well you swing it, you don't get very much momentum. In fact, when the ball hit it, your bat got knocked back by the pitch! It almost looked like the bat was going to get knocked out of your hands."

"It almost did!" I said, relieved that I could blame everything on the bat. "What a stupid bat!"

"Right," said Mr. Asher. "And balsa wood is spongy, so it absorbs energy. If you throw a ball against a hard wall, it bounces back. But if you throw it against a pillow, it just stops. That bat is like a pillow."

"Thanks a lot," I huffed. "So I guess I should have picked bat number three, right?"

"Well, let's find out. Since you were cheated just now, why don't you give it a try?"

"Oh, no," I said quickly. "I don't want to be greedy. Fernando there hasn't had a turn yet."

Mr. Asher turned to Fernando. "Okay, what about it, son?"

"Oh, I, um . . ." Fernando stammered. "Actually, do you have a bathroom here? I really have to go. Bad."

"Sure," said Mr. Asher. "Out the door we came in, and to the right. But don't be gone too long!" Fernando hurried out the door. He gave me a quick thumbs-up and a wink as he left. That told me Nando was actually off to do some Super Crew snooping.

"C'mon, I'm falling asleep out here!" yelled PJ.

"Well, how about you, Slugger?" Mr. Asher looked at Derek. "I think a crack hitter like you could really appreciate this." He held up the last baseball bat for all of us to admire.

"What is it?" I asked.

"What is it?" he exclaimed. "Why, this is a Hueyville Slugger! One of my own meticulously crafted bats! Composed of the finest ash wood. Sanded to perfection."

"Oh! A Hueyville Slugger!" I said enthusiastically. "Of course! The best wooden bat made. I didn't recognize it at first. It's so . . . beautifully bat-shaped." That was close. I nearly blew our cover, but my buttering-up seemed to work.

Mr. Asher beamed with pride. "And with this," he said, holding the bat up like a trophy, "our crack hitter shouldn't have any trouble at all hitting the ball into the stands." He pointed to the three walls painted with smiling faces.

Derek heaved a big sigh. "I don't know, Mr. Asher," he said. "It might take me a little while to get used to a new bat."

"Pshaw," said Mr. Asher. "As soon as you swing this bat of mine, you'll know that this is the bat you've always wanted to hit with. Try it." Mr. Asher held out the bat with both hands, like it was the most valuable prize in the world.

Derek reluctantly took it and walked to home plate. Mr. Asher walked out toward the pitcher's mound. "Okay, Pee-wee," he said. "Why don't you take a break and let me pitch a few?"

"But Mr. Asher, I was just getting warmed up!" PJ protested.

"Warmed up, huh? Looked to me like you were getting worn out. Those last couple of pitches you threw were marshmallows!"

"But—"

"No 'buts' about it, miss," Mr. Asher said sternly. "Derek here needs some real fastballs if he wants to really smack the ball. That's the other part of the science of baseball I was telling you about: the faster the pitch, the harder you can hit it."

"Derek's so good, he doesn't need a fast-ball!" I cried. "In fact, he specializes in hitting slow balls!"

"That isn't the point, Megan," said Mr. Asher, sounding a little impatient. "Imagine again that you're throwing a ball against a wall. Does it bounce back farthest if you throw it soft or hard?"

"Um, hard, I guess . . ." I answered.

"Exactly," he said conclusively. "And when my fastball is hit with a good, solid swing of a good, solid bat, it bounces back much farther than any slow pitch would. All right, Slugger, are you ready?" he shouted to Derek.

"As ready as I'll ever be," answered Derek, as confidently as he could manage. PJ and I walked behind Derek, close to the door—hoping that it was one place Derek would never hit the ball.

"Okay, then. Try *this*!"

Mr. Asher wound up and pitched. But the thing flew across the plate so fast that Derek didn't even have time to swing or think. The ball hit the backstop with a loud WHACK and actually got stuck in the chain-link mesh.

"Oh, sorry," Derek said, looking behind him at the ball like "how did that get there?"

"Weren't you watching?" Mr. Asher asked, looking at Derek with confusion.

"Um, not really," Derek said, trying to look at ease. "It's this bat. It feels so great. I forgot to swing."

"Oh," said Mr. Asher, breaking out into a grin. "I understand." Then he called out to PJ. "Toss me another ball, Pee-wee!"

PJ threw him a ball. He wound up and fired off another shot. Again, Derek didn't even have a chance to respond. The ball banked off the backstop and rolled back to Mr. Asher.

"Okay, big guy," Mr. Asher said, as he stooped to pick up the ball, "I'm beginning to think you're not a crack hitter at all."

This time, he threw a soft pitch right over the plate. But Derek swung too early. He completely missed the ball, and the force of his swing sent him spinning in place three times before coming to a stop.

Now we were really in for it. Mr. Asher couldn't possibly think we were baseball stars anymore.

"Your technique is excellent," said Mr. Asher.

"It is?" Derek asked with surprise.

"Yes," said Mr. Asher with a sour expression appearing on his face. "For a figure skater."

Ouch. Derek looked embarrassed, but PJ was determined to save our reputation.

"Can I take a turn with the Hueyville Slugger?" she asked hopefully.

"I don't think so," said Mr. Asher. "I think it's time to show you so-called baseball stars another piece of fine woodwork."

"Another bat?" I asked hopefully.

"No," he scowled, "the back door!"

Busted!

CHAPTER EIGHT

The Hour of Our Disk-content

While Derek was blowing our cover with the Hueyville Slugger, Fernando was sneaking through the halls of the factory, looking for any clues of sabotage to Boomer's bats. He didn't find much happening in the manufacturing unit. So he headed up to the main floor. After finding nothing more exciting than a candy machine, he finally came across a room labeled "computer lab." He put his ear to the door and overheard a conversation going on inside . . .

"You got all the specifications in order?" a man asked.

"Just putting the final changes in," said a woman. Fernando could hear the tapping of a keyboard. "This fella likes a real thick handle grip. Must have hands the size of the abominable snowman."

"Heh, heh," laughed the man. "C'mon. Let's go make sure they're coming out right at the other end."

Fernando jumped behind a water fountain as they left the room. When they were safely down the hall, Fernando snuck in. There were two large computers set up inside. One was displaying information about a current production project, the other one was turned on but paused at the main menu. Fernando glanced at the first computer but didn't touch it. If he did, he'd probably mess up somebody's custom order. And then the security guy would probably come mess *him* up!

Instead, he turned his attention to the second computer and scanned the list of menu headings. There he saw just what he wanted: Model Specifications. With a click of the mouse, he was into the Model Specifications file, with another click he was into an alphabetical listing of bat models, and with a final click he was into the file for the Babe Ruth bat. It was exactly the file we needed. Now we could find out if Boomer's bats had been sabotaged!

"Excellent!" Fernando said out loud, pushing his chair off from the computer table and rolling across the room. Then, in a move he'd mastered in the Control Car of the KC Express Train, he pushed off the wall, spun the chair around, and went zooming back toward the computer. This time, though, he lost control in the process. Instead of coming to a slow landing in front of his computer, he went flying into the first one— landing elbows-first on top of the keyboard.

"Oh no!" he cried, as the numbers on the screen in front of him started changing. He'd messed up the order! Downstairs, there were bats being made with 3 foot diameter grips. Weighing 36 pounds. Quickly, he tapped some keys and tried to recover the old information. But it was lost. To make matters worse, a loud alarm suddenly sounded out over the room's intercom. Somebody was onto him!

Quick as a flash, Fernando grabbed a blank

disk from a drawer and stuck it into the computer with the Babe Ruth bat file. He copied the information onto the disk, then snatched it back out. But just as he raced to leave the room, the door burst open and a big security guard dressed all in black stormed in.

"Put your hands in the air!" he yelled.

CHAPTER NINE

The Rescuers

While Fernando was having his adventures in the
computer lab, the rest of us were being escorted
out of the factory by Elton Asher. We tried a few
more stories about our love of baseball on him,
but he wasn't falling for it anymore. He had gone
from being wildly excited to wildly unhappy · · ·

"You kids, you're all the same," he said as he
shooed us out the door. "I thought you were
true-blue Americans who loved baseball and
great craftsmanship as much as I do."

"But we are," PJ insisted. "We do!"

He shook his head. "Goodbye, kids," he said,
closing the door. "I hope I never see you again."

He closed the door, leaving the three of us
sitting on the steps wondering what to do next.

"Wow. He was so mad he didn't even notice that Fernando's missing," Derek said.

"Fernando's missing?" I asked, looking around. "Oh. Right."

"Should we wait for him out here?" PJ asked.

"I think we should go in and find him," Derek said. "For all we know, he's gotten himself into trouble."

PJ tried the door. Fortunately, it was unlocked. So much for high security. After taking a quick peek to make sure Mr. Asher was out of sight, we slipped back inside.

"Now what?" I asked. "This place is huge. How do we find him?"

"Easy," PJ said. "I just heard his voice!"

She jogged down the hall, then paused to listen beside a closed door. When I caught up, I saw a sign on the door that said "SECURITY."

"Somebody just said something about torture!" PJ whispered, her ear pressed against the door. Torture? What were they doing to Fernando?

"Take that, you scum-sucking squid!" said a loud voice.

"Scum-sucking squid?" Derek said. "Why haven't I ever thought of calling him that?"

"Don't do it! Don't do it!" Fernando shrieked.

This was serious. Without wasting another moment, we burst into the room ready for anything. Fernando was sitting on a stiff-backed chair close to the door.

"Come on," PJ said, grabbing him by the arm. "Quick!"

"What are you doing?" cried the security guard, leaping up from his chair.

"He's with us," PJ said, tugging on Fernando's arm.

"No, he's with me," said the security guard, grabbing Fernando's other arm.

"No way," I said, "We aren't about to let you torture our friend!"

"Torture him?" asked the guard.

"What are you talking about?" Fernando said.

Suddenly I got the funny feeling that we'd made a big mistake. "You were in danger," I said.

"He called you a scum-sucking squid," Derek added.

"That wasn't us talking," the guard said, bursting into laughter. "That was the TV."

"Huh?" Derek asked.

"We were watching *The Outer Edge*," Fernando said. "Episode 305. My favorite! That is, until you burst in."

"Oops," I said.

"But you yelled, 'Don't do it!' " PJ said.

"Did I?" Fernando asked. "I guess I got excited. It's great watching with another fan."

"Another fan?" Derek asked.

"Yeah!" Fernando said. "Crew, meet Barney. He's the security guard here."

"I love *The Outer Edge*," explained Barney. "I watch it every day."

"I thought security guards were supposed to watch security monitors," I said.

"Oh, I videotape those while I'm watching the tube," said Barney. "Then I watch the tapes on high speed when my shows are over."

"That's nice," Derek said. "Now come on, Fernando, we have to go."

"You guys made me miss the end," Fernando moaned.

"Oh, well," Barney said, switching from TV to VCR and sliding a video into the machine. "At least now I can verify that you were just looking for the bathroom when I found you in the computer lab."

"Oh," said Fernando, looking suddenly worried. "The Crew's right. We'd better be going!"

With a panicked look on his face, he pushed us forward through the doorway and led us in a mad sprint for the front entrance.

"Hey, what are you doing back in here?" a voice cried out. It was Mr. Asher. He didn't look at all happy to see our faces again.

"I forgot my coat," I lied. "We're leaving! Promise!" I yelled as we dashed for the door.

"Stop them!" Barney the security guard shouted, racing after us.

But before he could catch up, we ran out the door, across the parking lot, and hopped aboard the KC Express Train.

"Giddyap, ALEC!" Fernando called into the Control Car. "Take us back to Kinetic City."

Once we were safely on our way, Fernando filled us in on what had happened to him. Apparently he'd tripped the security system on his chair-ride across the computer lab. When the security guy found him, Fernando had tried to convince him that he wasn't doing anything wrong—just looking for the bathroom. Of course, Barney wasn't sure if he should believe him. Fernando was trapped in the security office with the suspicious guard when, out of the blue, *The Outer Edge* came on the television. Barney was thrilled when he found out Fernando was a fellow fan of the show, so he happily put off interrogating Fernando until the program was over. Boy, did he get lucky!

We gave him a hard time about getting us into trouble. But he didn't want to hear it.

"You should thank me," he said. He reached into his jacket pocket. "I got this!" He held out a computer disk.

"What's that?" I asked.

"All the specs for Babe Ruth's bat!" Fernando said. "Once we compare this data to Boomer's bat, we can see if they match."

"And if they don't, we'll know somebody's been messing with Boomer's bats," Derek said.

"And if they *do* match," I said, "we'll know I was right all along."

CHAPTER TEN

Sizing Up the Situation

As we sped back to Kinetic City, we got ALEC ready to help us with our bat analysis. He was firing on all circuits when we told him how important this test was. Sometimes he reminds me of my little brother when I let him go to the store with me. ALEC always acts so grateful when we include him in our cases. I know, he's just programmed that way. But still, you have to admire his enthusiasm . . .

"Okay, Crew, let's have a look at that bat!" ALEC said cheerfully. As he spoke, a port opened up along the wall under his monitor. A metal arm whirred out of the port. In its grip was a hand-held scanner. "Just run that over the bat a few times so I can create a 3-D model of it for comparison," ALEC said.

Fernando grabbed the scanner and flipped it on. A red light glowed from the front. As he passed the scanner over the bat, a virtual bat appeared on ALEC's screen, along with numbers indicating its dimensions.

"Okay. Got it," ALEC said.

"Now let's do this," Fernando said, hitting a button so ALEC ejected a long metal tray, "and we can see how much this baby weighs."

He put the bat down on the tray.

"One moment," ALEC said, as lights flashed across his monitor. "Let's see. I'm getting a weight of forty-seven ounces."

"That's big for a bat," PJ said. "Maybe someone added weight to make it harder for Boomer to swing!"

"Let's see how it compares to Babe Ruth's bat," Fernando said. He popped his computer disk into ALEC's external drive.

Lights flashed as ALEC reviewed the data on the disk.

"Are you getting anything, ALEC?" PJ asked.

"One moment, please." Whirring sounds and little beeps followed, while we eagerly awaited his results. On his monitor another 3-D image of a bat appeared beside the first. "Finished!" ALEC said at last.

"Well?" Derek said eagerly. "Did you find any differences?"

"Yes!" Alec chimed.

"I knew it!" Derek yelled.

"Boomer's innocent!" PJ said.

I couldn't believe it! "Before you two break out the champagne . . ." I said. "ALEC, what's different about the bats? The grip? The weight?"

"No! Boomer's bats say 'Property of Boomer Baxter' on them," he beeped.

You should have seen Derek's and PJ's faces. "Oh, no!" they cried in unison.

"ALEC, that difference doesn't make any difference!" PJ said.

"You asked me to find any differences between the bats, and I did," ALEC said, sounding a bit hurt.

"Thank you, ALEC, you did a great job," I said, patting his screen. Then I turned to the Crew. "Now, can we get on with the *real* investigation?"

"Yeah," Fernando agreed. He checked his watch. "But let's get busy. The first game's already started!"

Derek sighed. "Okay. But remember. Until we know for sure that Boomer's cheating, we keep this completely quiet."

"No problem," I said.

But before we could do anything, a call came in on the KC Hotline.

"Kinetic City Super Crew," I said, picking up the phone. "When you want the facts—"

"Megan, this is Rudy Derosa. And yes, I'd like some facts."

"Hi, Mr. Derosa," I said. "What's up?" I tried to sound cool, but in truth I felt pretty nervous. We'd never been so far from solving a case with so little time left.

"Why didn't you kids call me back?" the manager asked.

"What? . . . Oh, no," I said. We had been so busy with the bats we hadn't noticed the flashing red message light on the hotline. He must have called while we were in the bat factory.

Mr. Derosa didn't wait for an excuse. "I can't believe you told the press before you told me," he said.

"Told them what?" I asked, surprised by the question. As far as I could remember, all we'd said to the press was a whole heap of "no comments."

"Told them about Boomer cheating!" Mr. Derosa replied angrily.

"What?" I asked. "We didn't say that!" I looked anxiously at the rest of the Crew. They could tell something alarming was going on.

"Maybe you'll remember when I quote you," Mr. Derosa said. "Here it is. The front page of the *Kinetic City Gazette*. In a headline, no less. 'SUPER CREW SAYS BOOMER'S THROWING THE GAMES!'"

For a moment I was stunned silent. "But we—"

"Listen, I can't talk anymore," Mr. Derosa said. "Sally Frost is waiting to see me. I think she wants to kill me."

"Why? What did you do?" I asked.

"What did *I* do? I told Boomer I was going to fire him!" Mr. Derosa said. "He was cheating!"

"No he wasn't! I mean, maybe he was, but we don't . . ." My mind was racing too fast to talk straight. "You can't do that yet. We don't have any proof!" I blurted.

"What did you say?" Mr. Derosa asked.

"The paper misquoted us," I said. "We, I mean *I*, thought he might be cheating, but we don't know that for sure."

"I think you'd better get down here, quick," Mr. Derosa said. "If we don't straighten this out soon, there's going to be a riot. This place is filling up with some angry fans, reporters are everywhere, Sally Frost is on the warpath, and Boomer's packing up his gear for good!"

"We'll be right there," I said. I hung up the phone and slumped into a chair.

The Crew knew something was really wrong.

"What is it, Megan?"

"What's going on?"

"What happened?"

I looked at them blankly. "Oops," I said.

CHAPTER ELEVEN

The Rockets' Red Glare

Mr. Derosa's phone call really knocked us for a loop. I couldn't believe those reporters had twisted our words like that! Derek tried to put on his "I told you so" act, but I told him to lay off. I knew the whole city would go nuts if we proved Boomer was cheating, I just didn't expect it to happen before we closed the case! The one person who could give us the answers we needed, besides Boomer, was Sally Frost. There was no time to do any more digging into her past. We had to confront her right now. After we picked up a copy of the Gazette at a newsstand to see for ourselves how bad the situation was, we made fast tracks for KC stadium . . .

"This isn't what I said," PJ said sadly, staring in disbelief at the newspaper.

I read over her shoulder. " 'Boomer was innocent until we proved him guilty,' said one Crew member."

"I can't believe they printed this stuff," Derek said.

Once we got to the stadium, we saw what Rudy Derosa was talking about. Only about half the seats were full. But the people who were there were going crazy. They were jeering and yelling and throwing stuff on the field. The first game of the double-header was almost over, and the Rockets were trying their best to just play. But it wasn't easy. A bunch of angry fans chanted, "Boomer, Boomer, he's the worst! If he weren't playing, we'd be first!" They didn't seem to notice that Boomer wasn't even in the game and the Rockets were still losing.

"I hope Boomer hasn't tried to leave yet," Derek said. "These people look like they could eat him alive."

"It's all our fault," said PJ sadly.

"Maybe we should look on the bright side," Fernando said. "Maybe Boomer really is guilty."

"There is no bright side, Fernando," Derek said. "That article was terrible."

"You can say that again," said a voice behind us.

We turned around to see Sally Frost standing beside us. She was furious.

"So," she said. "Are you proud of yourselves?" Her pale face had turned completely red. "You've just ruined the career of the nicest man in sports."

"Wait a second, Ms. Frost," I said. "We really need to talk to you."

"Haven't you done enough talking?" Sally Frost hissed. "Or would you like to spread some more lies?"

I wanted to explain how the reporters exaggerated, but there wasn't time. I had to get to the truth. "We know all about your secret deal," I blurted out.

Her red face got even redder. "What are you talking about?" she asked.

"We found the letter you wrote to Boomer, Ms. Frost," PJ said quietly. "We know you're involved."

"Well of course I'm involved!" Sally exclaimed. "I'm his agent! I'm involved in every deal Boomer makes!"

We were all stunned. Sally Frost had just confessed!

"I don't know how you snoops found out about this, but I'll make sure you pay. Your little detective agency, or whatever it is, is finished!" Then she turned on her heels and stormed for the exit.

"So much for that mystery," I said.

"I can't believe she just admitted it like that," PJ said.

"Unbelievable," said Fernando.

"I don't know . . ." Derek said.

"What's not to know, Derek?" I said. "Sally Frost is a mean old worm who used Blizzard Creek Hailstones' money to pay Boomer to throw games."

"So the Hailstones would make the playoffs," Fernando added.

"Really? I didn't hear her say that," Derek said.

"What do you mean? You were standing right there!" Fernando said.

"Yeah. And I heard Sally Frost admit to being in on a secret deal. But nobody said anything about payoffs or throwing games."

"You're crazy, Derek," I said.

"You guys!" PJ exclaimed. "Cut it out. We tried, but it's too late to do anything now. We just didn't have enough time."

"PJ's right," Fernando said. "If Boomer really was cheating, then he's already been fired and all these people have a reason to be mad. If he wasn't, we still don't know how to fix his hitting. Besides, I don't think Rudy Derosa would send him out there to be devoured by those fans, anyway. We just have to hope the Rockets can win one of these games without Boomer's help."

"That job just got a little harder," Derek said. "Look." He pointed down on the field. The first game was over. The ninth inning had ended with a Blue Sox double-play and another loss for the Rockets. The half-empty stands began to empty even more.

"Oh no," PJ moaned.

I was about to give in and admit defeat, but then something truly weird happened.

"Look!" Fernando yelled as he pointed to the field. "It's Boomer!"

CHAPTER TWELVE

Boomer Strikes Out

The middle of left field was absolutely the last place any of us thought we'd see Boomer Baxter. With practically the whole city after his skin, we figured he was in serious hiding. But there he was, dressed in his uniform, holding a cardboard box under his arm. Next to him was an older man holding a microphone in one hand, and what looked like a TV remote in the other. It was Al Charboni, the owner of the Grand Slam Grill, in the same blue suit he was wearing when we met him passing out flyers the day before . . .

"What's going on?" I asked. "Is Boomer going to apologize?"

"No, I think it has to do with that contest Mr. Charboni told us about," Derek said.

"Oh yeah!" Fernando said. "Let's stay, you guys. I want to see if I win."

"I want to see why Boomer is out there," PJ said.

Mr. Charboni flipped on the microphone and his voice filled the stadium. "Hey there, Rockets fans! Don't go anywhere just yet! I'm Al Charboni, founder and owner of the Grand Slam Grill. How 'bout those Rockets!" He paused for applause, but instead a chorus of boos filled the stadium.

"All right!" Mr. Charboni said. He looked like he was trying his best to stay cheerful. It couldn't have been easy. Now that he had drawn people's attention to the field, they were slowly beginning to realize that Boomer was down there. "Now let's get down to business! In my hand I hold the remote control switch that will raise the brand new Grand Slam Grill sign into place above the left field wall! And one of you will get to come down here and do the honors!"

More boos. Poor Mr. Charboni. It wasn't his fault the Rockets' season had nosedived. There was nothing he could do but keep right on going.

"And now, to draw the name of our lucky winner, and to help introduce our exciting new menu item, please give a big welcome to the Home-Run King himself, Mr. Boomer Baxter!"

This was completely bizarre. Al Charboni had picked the most despised man in Kinetic City to be in his ceremony! Nobody could believe it. The crowd went totally ape. They screamed and booed and threw everything they could get their hands on. A group above the dugout broke into a chant. "Boomer, Boomer, he's the worst! When he's around, this team is cursed!"

"This is too embarrassing to watch," I said.

Boomer looked like a prisoner waiting for the firing squad. He stepped up to the microphone with his head down and pulled a piece of paper from his pocket. Then he cleared his throat and read his lines like he was reading numbers out of a phone book. We could barely hear him over the screaming crowd.

"Thank you, Mr. Charboni. I'm thrilled to be here in front of all you Rockets fans to help unveil your new sign. I'm also very excited to tell everyone about the Grand Slam Grill's . . . mouth-watering . . . new menu item." He paused and took a deep breath. "The Boomer Burger! Yes, this delicious . . ." his voice trailed off and he took a big gulp, "all-beef patty is sure to touch all the bases of your appetite and send you home with a smile on your face."

The crowd groaned.

"I can't believe he's doing this," Derek said.

"Boomer, Boomer, he's the worst!" the rowdy ones continued.

"What do you know about touching all the bases?" a fan yelled out.

Luckily, Boomer was too far away to hear any specific comments. But the boos that filled the air must have stung like bee stings. Somehow he kept plowing head. He took another deep breath and broke into song in a weak and off-key voice,

> *"Take me out for a new taste.*
> *Take me out for a meal.*
> *The new Boomer Burger just can't be beat*
> *I guarantee it's a great hunk of meat!*
> *Oh, it's juice, juice, juicy and flame-broiled.*
> *I know it will give you a thrill!*
> *For it's one, two, three times the beef*
> *At the Grand Slam Grill!"*

Now the boos and jeers were louder than ever. Mr. Charboni took back the microphone. His face looked like all the color had drained right out of it. This was not going the way he had planned. "Thank you, Boomer. Now let's draw the name of our lucky winner."

"Oh, this is terrible," Derek said.

"Yeah. Someone should have given Boomer some acting and singing lessons," Fernando said.

"That's not the terrible thing," Derek said. "Boomer's a vegetarian. Getting up there and endorsing an all-beef patty must go against everything he believes in! I can't believe he'd do this. Forget throwing games; selling out like this is ten times worse in my book."

"Yeah," PJ said. "He should be selling beet and tofu casserole."

Suddenly I got a sinking feeling in my stomach. "Oh no," I said.

"What's the matter, Megan?" Fernando asked. "Is thinking about that casserole grossing you out?"

"No," I said. "But think about what Derek just said. Standing up there and singing the Grand Slam Grill jingle goes against everything Boomer believes in."

"It's ugly what some people will do for money, isn't it?" Fernando said.

"But don't you see?" I said. "Those are just the words Boomer used yesterday. On the phone. When I thought he was talking to Sally Frost or someone else from Blizzard Creek about losing the game!"

"What are you saying, Megan?" PJ asked.

"I'm saying maybe he wasn't talking to Sally Frost. If you think about it, he could have easily been talking to Al Charboni about doing this Boomer Burger thing," I said.

"Sure," Fernando said, piecing it together now. "Didn't he say something like, 'Tomorrow night. I'm your man?'"

I nodded. It had to be true. Boomer wasn't talking to anyone about throwing the game. He was just feeling guilty about endorsing a hamburger!

"Is this where I get to say 'I told you so?'" Derek said smugly.

"The secret deal Sally Frost admitted to. This was it, wasn't it?" I said.

"I'd bet anything," Derek said.

"Oh, brother," PJ said. "We got Boomer fired for nothing."

"Well come on, Crew! Let's get moving," Fernando said. "We still have time to sort this out."

We were interrupted from Fernando's pep talk by the desperate voice of Al Charboni. "DOESN'T ANYONE WANT TO COME DOWN HERE AND PUSH THIS SWITCH?" he yelled. "PLEASE!"

"What's going on?" PJ asked.

"I think Mr. Charboni's big contest is going up in smoke," Derek said. "Look at all those entry forms." He was right. Little slips of paper were blowing all over the field.

While we had been talking, Boomer had drawn name after name from the box, but nobody had actually come down to claim the prize. They were all too mad at Boomer. Who could blame them? They all thought he was a cheater. Then suddenly, I had an idea!

"Crew, we have to get down there, right now!" I said.

"To raise the Grand Slam Grill sign?" Fernando asked.

"No, to tell everybody Boomer didn't cheat!" I said. "We can announce it on the P.A. system."

"Good idea, Megan," Derek said. "We have to do something to get this place under control."

"Okay," PJ said. "Let's go!"

CHAPTER THIRTEEN

A Special Announcement

We made our way down to the dugout and explained to Rudy Derosa what we had figured out. Once we told him we were sure Boomer was innocent, he looked a little confused, but he said it was okay if we tried to tell the crowd about the whole mixed-up mess. We ran out to left field, but it turned out we weren't the first ones to have that idea. A pack of reporters had already crowded around Boomer and Mr. Charboni. Sally Frost was there trying to get Boomer off the field, and a couple of security guards were nervously keeping an eye on the fans to make sure none of them tried to join the party . . .

"Boomer, Boomer, he's a geek! Just go back to Blizzard Creek!" chanted a couple of rowdy guys up in the stands. To drive their point home, they unfurled a big white sheet with "Boomer go home" spray-painted on it. The sheet flapped in the wind like a sail.

"Are you sure you want to try to talk to these wackos?" Derek asked me.

This was definitely not going to be a receptive audience.

"Mr. Charboni!" one of the reporters said as we got closer. "What were you thinking when you chose Boomer to endorse your new burger?"

"What was I thinking?" Mr. Charboni exclaimed. "I was thinking that Boomer Baxter is the greatest player the Rockets have ever had. Putting his name on a burger was great marketing!"

"But Boomer's been disgraced by a cheating scandal," another reporter pointed out. "Don't you read the papers?"

"Yes I do," Mr. Charboni responded. "But I thought that story was a bunch of hooey.

Boomer's a real stand-up guy. Honest as the day is long. I figured you media sharks made the whole thing up to sell some papers. Besides, I arranged this whole ceremony weeks ago. The sign was made, the flyers were printed. It was too late to turn back, if you know what I mean."

"Boomer, what do you have to say in your defense?" a reporter asked. "Did you do it? Did you really throw the games so Blizzard Creek would make the playoffs?"

Boomer started to answer, but Sally Frost jumped in. "How dare you even suggest that my client is anything but the victim of a horrible smear campaign, spread by those miserable children!"

All eyes suddenly turned to look at us.

"It's the Super Crew," one reporter said. "Crew, is it true? Did you make up the whole story to run Boomer out of town?"

This was getting way out of hand! "No!" I cried. "You've got it all wrong! You have to let us explain!"

"Oh, this should be good," Sally Frost groaned.

I walked over to Mr. Charboni and reached for the microphone. "May I?" I asked.

"Sure," he said. "This whole ceremony is a bust. I give up."

I looked over at the Crew. They all gave me a thumbs-up. I noticed the TV cameras were pointing right at me. I was about to go live to the whole city! "Hello, Kinetic City," I said. My voice rang around the stadium. I cleared my throat and kept going. "I'm Megan, from the Kinetic City Super Crew, and I have something very important to say. So if you could all just listen for a minute, I'd appreciate it."

The boos seemed to quiet a bit, so I went on. "As you all know, there was an article in the *Gazette* today that quoted the Super Crew. It said we proved Boomer Baxter was throwing games by pretending to be in a hitting slump."

Another round of jeers and catcalls circled the stadium. "I am here now to tell you that that story you read was completely false." That got them. The angry shouts suddenly turned to a low rumble of confusion. "We were misquoted. Boomer Baxter is *not* a cheater," I said. "So let's just put this whole silly affair behind us and play ball! Thank you!"

I didn't get quite the enthusiastic response I was hoping for from the crowd, but at least they had calmed down a bit. They were still pretty confused, I guess. But now everyone knew that Boomer was innocent. There was just one little problem.

"I still can't hit home runs," Boomer said. "Unless you kids came up with an answer for me."

"Sorry, Boomer," PJ said. "We tried. But . . ."

Suddenly Fernando yelled, "Look out!" Then before we knew what was happening, a huge white piece of fabric dropped over us like a net.

"Hey, what's going on?" I yelled.

"It's that sheet those guys were waving," PJ said. "The one that said 'Boomer go home' on it."

Mr. Charboni and a couple of security guards ran over and helped us pull the sheet off.

"Hey, you losers!" I shouted to the guys in the stands, "why'd you do that?"

"Sorry, man," one of the fans said, "the wind just blew it out of our hands."

"Yeah, right," Fernando said.

"No, really," the guy said. "It's like a tornado up here!"

"But it was pretty funny when it landed on you guys," the other fan laughed.

"Oh, yeah. Hilarious," I said. I turned back to Boomer, but the reporters had swarmed around him again.

"So Boomer," a reporter asked, "now that your name has been cleared, are you ready to play?"

"I don't think so," Boomer said sadly. "I still can't hit home runs. I thought I just needed some time, but time's in short supply right now. Maybe if the Super Crew had figured out what was wrong with me, I'd be ready. But they didn't—and I'm not."

"Actually, Boomer, we *did* figure it out." Everybody turned around to see Derek holding the big sheet and smiling.

"We did?" I asked.

"Sure we did," Derek said, pointing to the sheet. "The answer's right here."

" 'Boomer go home?' " Fernando asked.

"No, not that," Derek said. "The wind blew this down here!"

"That's right," Sally Frost said. "We already know that."

"Hold on," Derek said. "Crew, remember when we got caught in the sprinklers, and the wind kept blowing the water in our eyes?"

"Yeah, how could I forget?" I said.

"And remember what ALEC said about the winds that blow off the water? They blow over this place at a constant thirty-five miles an hour."

"Where are you going with this, young man?" Mr. Charboni asked.

"I know!" PJ said. "The wind is the cause of Boomer's slump! It's blowing his hits back into the outfield. The ball's being knocked out of the sky!"

"Now wait a minute," said one of the reporters. "Are you trying to tell me that

Boomer is suddenly being affected by the wind? Because it's the same wind that's here every day. It was here all season long when he was hitting the homers without a problem."

"I know," said Derek. "But something happened two weeks ago that changed things."

"Yeah! Boomer started getting out!" said one of the reporters.

"And—" Derek began.

"And Mr. Derosa took down the Grand Slam Grill sign!" Fernando said, finishing Derek's thought. "It was right there, over right field. It must have been blocking the wind!"

"Exactly," Derek said, smiling. "And with nothing there to replace it, the wind blew in over right field like a tornado. Just like those guys said up in the stands."

"That doesn't make sense. Why didn't any of the other players notice the change?" another reporter asked.

"Because Boomer's the only lefty on the team," PJ said. "Right, Boomer?"

"Right," Boomer said. "I hit all over the field like anybody else. But when I really connect for a home-run blast I almost always pull it to right field."

"And Boomer hits so many more homers than anybody else, it really got noticed when he stopped knocking them over the wall," PJ said.

"Wait a minute," Sally Frost said. "Are you saying my client's season went to pieces because HE took down his shabby old burger ad?" She pointed a long finger at Al Charboni.

Mr. Charboni looked uncomfortable. "I never knew it was doing any good. I thought it was just dropping paint chips in the stands."

"So what do we do now?" Fernando said

"I think Mr. Charboni is holding the answer in his hand," I said.

He looked down at the remote switch. "The new sign!" he said. "Of course! Let's get that baby in place!"

"You might want this," I said as I handed over the microphone.

"Ladies and gentlemen!" Mr. Charboni bellowed through the P.A. "I give to you the new, improved, *wind blocking*, Grand Slam Grill sign!"

With a flip of a switch on his remote control, a creaking and rumbling of machinery began from the outside of the stadium. Slowly, above the right-field bleachers wall, a bright Rockets-red sign began to rise on a motorized platform. The crowd murmured and pointed as the two-story image of Boomer Baxter taking a big bite from a Boomer Burger rose above Kinetic City stadium. Finally, with a loud CHUNK, it locked into place. The neon light tubes around the sign's edge flickered then came to life with a rainbow of color. The crowd loved it. Mr. Charboni loved it. Everybody loved it.

Well, almost everybody . . .

CHAPTER FOURTEEN

Where's the Beef?

We headed back across the field toward the
dugout basking in the glow of another case
closed. Even Sally Frost let a crooked half-smile
cross her face once she realized we had figured
out the source of Boomer's slump. With Boomer's
name cleared and the Grand Slam Grill sign in
place, we figured the Rockets were almost
guaranteed to win the last game of the season
and secure a place in the playoffs. But, as we
reached the dugout, I noticed Boomer was acting
strangely. He should have been jumping with joy to
be free from his slump and from the fans' boos,
but instead he looked more depressed than ever . . .

"What's wrong, Boomer?" PJ asked.

"What's wrong?" he exclaimed. "That
stupid sign, that's what! I never should have
gone through with it."

"I thought the artist captured you per-fectly," Mr. Charboni said, a little defensively.

"That's not the problem," Boomer said. "I mean, singing that silly song was one thing. But to have to stare at that picture of me biting into that hamburger every time I step up to hit . . . Well, let's just say no amount of meditation will ever keep me focused with that thing looming over me."

"Yeah," Derek said with a scowl. "It must be hard to focus when you're going against everything you believe in."

"Derek, that's mean!" PJ said.

"No, Derek's right," Boomer said. "Just thinking about having a hamburger named after me makes me queasy."

"Then why'd you do it?" Derek asked. "Why did you sell out?"

"He didn't sell out!" Sally Frost broke in. "Boomer didn't take one penny of that endorse-ment deal for himself."

"What do you mean?" I asked.

"Boomer turned me down cold at first, because the Boomer Burger went against his conscience," Mr. Charboni said.

"Good. It should have," said Derek, looking relieved.

"What made him change his mind?" I asked.

"I gave him an idea for what to do with the money," said Ms. Frost. We all paused in silence as we awaited the explanation. "He was going to start a refuge for cattle. Where they could live free and not be turned into hamburger."

"Wow. That's so nice," PJ said.

"So that's what he does with his money," I said. "He buys refuges for cattle?"

"Well, he also has a home for stray cats," said Ms. Frost. "And an organic birdseed farm. And he built a gymnasium for the Blizzard Creek *and* Kinetic City orphanages. And he bought everyone in his family houses in Malibu. And he sent care packages to the entire country of Somalia . . ."

"Okay, okay!" Derek laughed. "We get the picture."

"So your conscience should be clear, Boomer!" PJ said. "What's a few burgers when you're practically saving the world?"

"You're right," Boomer said. "But it still bothers me. I mean, I'm telling people to eat something I wouldn't touch myself. And for every cow I save, another one is turned into a Boomer Burger!"

"Now see here, Boomer," Mr. Charboni growled. "We signed a contract. You can't go and get all wishy-washy on me again."

"Wait! I got it!" PJ yelled. "If you won't endorse a beef patty, why not make the Boomer Burger a vegi-burger?"

"A vegi-burger?" Mr. Charboni asked. "What are you talking about?"

"Wow! That's a great idea," Boomer said. "We can make it out of tofu. Or barley. Or organic kelp."

Mr. Charboni looked a little sick. "Now that's a sweet idea and all, Boomer. But who's ever going to eat a thing like that?"

For a moment there was silence. Then a Rockets player at the end of the bench piped up. "I would," he said.

A second later, another player called out. "I'd eat one of those. Maybe it would make me as strong as Boomer."

"Me, too," said Sally Frost. "And I'm not just saying that because Boomer's my client. Okay, maybe I am. But I still think it's a great idea."

"I'd eat one, too," PJ said.

"Me too," Derek said.

We looked at Fernando. "I'd . . . well . . . I'd smell one if you wanted me to," he finally said.

"Well, heck, why not?" Mr. Charboni said. "It'll be good to diversify the menu. And if selling a vegi-burger means Boomer will start hitting home runs again, well then by golly I'll sell vegi-burgers!"

The dugout erupted in cheers. The whole Rockets team looked happier than they had in weeks.

"Thanks Super Crew," Boomer said.

"No problem," I replied.

"I thought this slump was something I could solve by myself," Boomer said, "but you guys proved that sometimes you need a little teamwork."

The Rockets' manager overheard Boomer and came over. "I don't believe it!" Rudy Derosa laughed. "Boomer Baxter, the original lone wolf, admits he likes teamwork? Does that mean you'll go out for ribs and bowling with us tonight?"

"Uh . . ." Boomer said.

"He's busy," I jumped in. "He's helping Derek with his swing."

"What?" Derek asked.

"Oh, yeah, that's right," Boomer said, playing along. "Sorry, Rudy."

"You play?" Mr. Derosa asked Derek.

"Oh yeah," Fernando said before Derek could answer. "Derek's the next Boomer Baxter!"

"We call him Driller Derek!" PJ exclaimed.

Mr. Derosa's eyes lit up. "Really?" he said as he grabbed a bat. "We're about to start batting practice for the next game. Why don't you join us, Derek?"

"Oh no, not again!" Derek exclaimed.

PJ, Fernando, and I exchanged grins. Boomer was right. Teamwork *is* great!

CHAPTER FIFTEEN

No Place Like Home

We had a great time watching Derek talk his way out of batting practice and then we headed up to the stands to watch the Rockets try one last time to clinch their place in the playoffs. It was close for a couple of innings. But when Boomer came up to the plate, he watched a couple of pitches go by then he smashed a towering home run right into the new Grand Slam Grill sign! After that it was a romp. The Rockets cruised to an 8-2 win. The whole city celebrated for days afterward. After the game Rudy Derosa gave us a signed baseball from the team, and told us we were the greatest. Al Charboni promised us free burgers for life.

Boomer offered to take us with him to meditation camp. And Sally Frost apologized for calling us "drippy slackers."

All in all, one of our most high-profile cases had turned out amazingly well. We celebrated with the team for a while, then headed back to the KC Express Train, feeling happy and calm at last . . .

"This case was the best!" PJ said, tossing the autographed baseball into the air.

"Yeah," Derek agreed.

"And we wrapped up everything perfectly!" Fernando said, shoving off in his chair and rolling at record speed across the floor of the Control Car. He bounced off the wall and was flying back toward us when a loud knock sounded out at the side door.

Fernando got up and opened the door with a grin, probably expecting more free food. Instead, we saw Elton Asher, the Hueyville Slugger guy, standing in the parking lot with an absolutely enormous baseball bat in his arms.

The grip alone must have been three feet around! Behind him was a cart overflowing with more giant bats.

"Excuse me for bothering you," he said with a sour expression on his face. "But I believe you ordered these?"

Fernando stared at the bats in disbelief. "Uh oh," he said at last. "I'm in BIG trouble!"

THE END

GET REAL!

This and every *Kinetic City Super Crew* adventure is based on real science.

And the science involved in hitting a baseball into the stands is as complicated as putting a satellite in orbit.

Don't believe it? Well, first of all, you've got all that Isaac Newton physics stuff from Chapter 7. Hitting a ball hard means your bat needs to have much more *momentum* than the ball does. Remember momentum? It's a combination of speed (how fast you can swing the bat) and mass (how heavy your bat is).

Every batter wants to hit the ball with as much momentum as possible. Since every hitter is different when it comes to arm strength and quickness, there is no "ideal" bat for everyone. But baseball experts and scientists agree that bat speed is more important than mass. Why? If you take a bat that you can swing very fast, and then add even just 5 ounces, it will *really* slow down your swing. That slowness weakens your hitting more than the extra few ounces help it.

The other problem with a big bat is control. To be a good hitter you have to make tiny but important adjustments as you make your swing. Heavy bats have more *inertia* (that's more Newton! It's pronounced "in-ER-sha"). Inertia is how Newton described the way really heavy things are hard to get moving; and how, once they're moving, it's hard to stop them or make them change direction. And, of course, the most important thing in hitting is making good contact with the ball. So if a heavy bat has so much inertia that you can't adjust the swing enough to hit that curve ball, the mass of a big bat won't do you much good.

Some famous hitters have admitted that they "doctored" their bats to help them hit better, even though that's against Major League Baseball rules. Over the years, players have drilled long holes down the barrel of the bat, from the top, and stuck cork in the hole. Cork is a springy, spongy kind of wood, and the batters think that it can make the baseball spring off their bat more.

But scientists think it's a dumb idea, since soft cork in the bat would just absorb more energy from the ball, and make any hit weaker. And since the cork is buried so deeply in the bat, it might not have any effect at all. Yet some hitters swear that it works. It's possible that by drilling out the hardwood, and putting in cork, they just made their bat lighter, and were able to swing it faster and with more control. Maybe that's why they got more hits. They probably should have just tried a lighter bat.

One more bit of Newton: He noticed that for every *action*, there is an equal and opposite *reaction*. So when a bat hits a ball with a certain force (we'll call that the action), the exact same force hits the bat, pushing it backward (the reaction). Of course, when bat meets ball, hitters want the ball to move forward (it's pretty embarrassing to have the bat blown out of your hands). Fortunately, they use bats that have much more mass than baseballs do. So the same force that makes the baseball fly into the stands has hardly any effect on the motion of the bat, because the bat has more momentum. If the baseball had more mass (let's imagine you play in a league where giants throw cannon balls), then it's the bat that would go flying.

There's one more great big factor involved in hitting a baseball that not even rocket scientists sending satellites though space have to worry about: air. You can't see it, but it really affects how a baseball moves. By spinning the ball a certain way, or not putting any spin on it at all, pitchers can make the baseball move in unexpected ways, so it's hard to hit. That's because the seams of the baseball can push against the air. Changing how those seams spin through the air can really change the path of the ball.

And, as the Super Crew learned, air currents in the ballpark can also affect hitting. Candlestick Park in San Francisco is near the ocean and is famous for having crazy winds. That can be tough on hitters. A head wind of just 10 miles per hour can turn what would otherwise be a 400-foot home run into a 370-foot hit—which most outfielders will catch.

The ideal place for hitters to hit would be a ballpark with no air at all (except for the suffocating and dying part). Not only would curve balls not curve, but wind wouldn't affect their fly balls, and there would be no "friction" or air resistance. That's when the baseball slows down because it's bumping against air molecules.

There aren't any "no air" ballparks in Major League Baseball (maybe someday there will be one on the moon), but Coors Field in Denver, Colorado, is the next best thing. It's so high above sea level that the air is very thin, and baseballs fly . . . well, almost like rockets.

HOME CREW
HANDS ON

Hey, Home Crew—

After our adventure with the KC Rockets, I realized that the science of sports is pretty amazing. Once you start thinking about action and reaction, you realize that lots of different things can affect the way players play: the size and weight of the equipment, the wind, the athlete's strength and timing, how many fries they ate that morning, and much, much, more.

PJ told me she thought that air temperature is a big deal, too. She claimed hot or cold temperatures don't just affect how much athletes sweat; she thought they also change the way the ball handles.

I wasn't so sure of that. I mean, nonliving things like baseballs and basketballs don't feel the air temperature, do they? I mean, who ever saw a basketball shiver?

Derek said instead of arguing about this, we should figure out a way to test PJ's idea. So here's what we did:

We took two brand-new tennis balls out of a can. We put one ball outside, where it was about 70 degrees Fahrenheit. And we put the other one in the freezer. Four hours later, we had one warm tennis ball and one very frozen tennis ball.

Then we did a test to see if the balls bounced differently. PJ got a yardstick from the Workshop Car. Then we went outside on the sidewalk and she held the yardstick with one end on the ground and the other straight up in the air. Then she held the warm tennis ball at exactly three feet, and let it drop on the ground. Meanwhile, I was crouching down next to the yardstick so I could see how high the ball bounced. We did this ten times, and I wrote down all the heights on a piece of paper. To get an average bounce, we added all the heights together and divided by ten.

Then we got the frozen ball out of the freezer and repeated the same steps. PJ dropped the ball ten times and I recorded the heights ten times. Then we added these heights together and divided by ten again.

Now we had the average bounce height for the warm tennis ball and the average bounce height for the frozen tennis ball. Do you think they were the same? Different? I'm not telling! You'll just have to do the experiment for yourself.

All you need are two tennis balls. Put one in the freezer—for at least three hours. And leave the other outside or, if it's cold outside, in your warm house. Then measure the bounces of each ball the same way PJ and I did. (Make sure you're bouncing the balls on a hard surface—the experiment won't work well on carpeting or grass.) What's your average bounce for each ball?

And now, for the really big question: Can you explain why this happened?

When you finish your experiment and come up with an explanation, give us a call. You can reach us at our Web site at www.kineticcity.com.

Or, you can call us on the phone at 1-800-877-CREW. That's 1-800-877-2739.

Okay, Home Crew? Now, PLAY BALL!

Your friend,

Megan

Puzzle Pages

PJ's Math Across

Hey Home Crew,

Baseball has always been a game of numbers, and real hardball nuts like me always have a crazy pile of statistics in our heads. On the next page are some baseball facts and figures I came up with for you to fill in. Match the lettered clues to the boxes in the grid I made. Once you have all the numbers in place, every row of numbers—from left to right and from the top down—will be a mathematical equation. Fill in the answers you know and do the math to fill in the clues you can't answer off the top of your head.

Good Luck!

PJ

A	≠	B	−	C	=	D
≠	■	−	■	−	■	×
E	×	F	+	G	=	H
−	■	−	■	≠	■	−
I	+	J	×	K	=	L
=	■	=	■	=	■	=
M	−	N	−	O	=	7

A: The distance between the bases is ____ ft.

B: There are ___ innings in a normal game.

C: All the spectators stand up for the ____th inning stretch.

D: Babe Ruth's uniform number was ____.

E: and F: A full count is _____ balls and ____ strikes.

G: ____ strikes and you're out.

H: ____ players take the field.

I: There are ____ teams in the American League.

J: ____ runs score on a grand slam.

K: The Kansas City Royals have won ____ World Series.

L: The Cleveland Indians won the World Series in 19____ and 1948.

M: There are ____ teams in the National League.

N: Each team gets ____ outs per inning.

O: A hitter walks after ____ balls.

Answers on page 160.

Grand Slam Scramble

Unscramble the words in Megan's notes so she can file them in the Case Closed drawer.

1) The more (NETMMOMU) _ _ _ _ _ _ _ _
   a baseball has, the farther it goes $\quad\overline{1}$
   when you hit it.

2) Major League baseball bats are made of
   (HAS) _ _ _ wood.
   $\quad\quad\quad\overline{9}$

3) Before he played for the Rockets, Boomer
   Baxter lived in (ZADBIZLR ERKEC)

   _ _ _ _ _ _ _ _ _ _ _ _ _.
   $\quad\overline{5}\quad\quad\quad\quad\quad\quad\overline{8}$

4) Elton Asher made Hugheyville (EGSLGUR)

   _ _ _ _ _ _ _ bats.
   $\quad\quad\overline{6}$

5) The 1919 Chicago team that got caught
   cheating were known as the (KALBC OSX)

   _ _ _ _ _ _ _ _.
   $\quad\quad\overline{3}$

6) How a baseball stadium is (GNEDSIED)
   _ _ _ _ _ $\frac{}{7}$ _ _ has a lot to do with how
   much the wind affects the game.

7) Even if two things are the same size, if one
   has more (ASMS) $\frac{}{4}$ _ _ _ it will weigh
   more.

8) Winds that blow consistently from the same
   direction are known as (VREPLAIIGN)
   _ _ $\frac{}{2}$ _ _ _ _ _ _ _ winds.

Now fill in the blanks below with the numbered
letters to complete this sentence:

The Super Crew used great $\frac{}{1} \frac{}{2} \frac{}{3} \frac{}{4}$ work to
help $\frac{}{5} \frac{}{3} \frac{}{6} \frac{}{7} \frac{}{8} \frac{}{9}$ the Rockets into the playoffs!

Answers on page 161.

Change-Up

Change one letter in each of the words below to make a list of baseball terms.

1. Bull   _____
2. But   _____
3. Bake   _____
4. Hound   _____
5. Mist   _____
6. Grove   _____
7. Stripe   _____
8. Talk   _____
9. Steak   _____
10. Pinch   _____
11. Bust   _____
12. Carve   _____
13. Soul   _____

Answers on page 161.

Action Reaction

Find a chair that rolls and place it on a smooth, hard surface. Grab something heavy but soft, like a grocery bag full of magazines, then sit in the chair. Throw the bag out in front of you with both hands, as hard as you can. What is the reaction to your action? If you do it right, you should roll backward as the bag moves forward. When you push against the heavy bag, it pushes back against you, sending you rolling away.

SuperCrew instant ideas

just add brain power and stir

Hot Stuff

When a pitcher throws a strike, they say he's "throwing heat." It's not just a silly term. As the ball is thrown, it rubs against the air, causing friction. This rubbing generates heat—not enough to actually feel when you catch the ball, but it's there. All friction makes heat. It's a law of physics. Rub your hands together quickly and feel them warm up. That's friction at work.

Answers

PJ's Math Across

A 90	≠	**B** 9	−	**C** 7	=	**D** 3
≠		−		−		×
E 3	×	**F** 2	+	**G** 3	=	**H** 9
−		−		≠		−
I 16	+	**J** 4	×	**K** 1	=	**L** 20
=		=		=		=
M 14	−	**N** 3	−	**O** 4	=	7

Grand Slam Scramble

1. Momentum
2. Ash
3. Blizzard Creek
4. Slugger

5. Black Sox
6. Designed
7. Mass
8. Prevailing

The Super Crew used great teamwork to help launch the Rockets into the playoffs!

Change-Up

1. Ball
2. Bat
3. Base
4. Mound
5. Mitt
6. Glove
7. Strike

8. Walk
9. Steal
10. Pitch
11. Bunt
12. Curve
13. Foul

Other Case Files

From **U.F. uh-Oh:**
The Case of the Mayor's Martians

We all hopped in the Desert Rover and sped around to the other side of Mount Squashmore. It took longer than I thought. Between Area 15 and the mountain itself, there was a lot to circle around. The sand flying in our faces didn't make it any easier. But I felt like I had to see what those "flying saucers" really were.

I didn't really know what to expect. After that weird tour and the slimy goo in the closet, some part of my mind couldn't help thinking that the alien story might just be real. Or at least that something creepy was going on. But the no-nonsense, scientific part told me not to jump to conclusions. I guess both parts really wanted to see what this thing was.

As it turned out, neither of them would get the chance. When we finally turned the corner behind the mountain, we saw a couple of familiar faces. It was Lars and Louie, the guys in the dark suits and sunglasses who had towed Stacy back to Kinetic City. This time, they were in a different *truck. It looked like a moving van, except it was black like the tow truck. And it looked like they had just packed away whatever had landed back there . . .*

"Excuse me!" Keisha firmly but politely called out to the agents. "Lars? Louie? It's us, the Kinetic City Super Crew." She flashed her Super Crew ID card just to keep it legit.

"That's right," Megan said. "We're the Mayor's special guests, remember?"

"No," said Lars in his flattest monotone.

"Don't be silly, Lars," Louie said. He turned to us. "He's a kidder, Lars is. Great sense of humor." Lars just stared straight ahead with a steely scowl. "Of course we remember you. How was your tour, folks?"

"Very enlightening," Mr. Snerr said. "But the best part was the end. We saw some flying saucers land in this very spot!"

"What?" Louie asked. Lars frowned.

"What he means is, did anything just land out here?" I explained. "Something metal? On a parachute?"

"No," Lars replied firmly.

"That's right!" Louie added. "Nothing's landed back here since, well . . . I can't remember, because it probably never happened!"

"Quiet, Louie," Lars snarled.

"No, really," Fernando insisted. "We just saw something come out of the sky. It should have landed right around here."

I felt like being bold. "You're not hiding it, are you?"

"No," said Lars.

"Absolutely not!" Louie chimed in. "If you saw something, it was probably really boring. Even if something did land out here, and we had it in the truck right now, you wouldn't want to look at it."

"Actually, we kinda would," Megan said. "Can we take a peek?"

"No," said Lars.

"That's right! There's no reason to look in the truck," Louie chirped. "We just happened to be driving by here. This metal thing that's in our truck right now has nothing to do with the thing you saw. Or the Mayor. Or some secret of his. Or aliens."

"Wait a second. We didn't mention the Mayor. Or some secret of his. Or aliens," I said suspiciously.

"And you just said you had something metal in the truck," Snerr noted.

Lars flashed Louie a glare that would melt concrete. "Get in the truck, Louie," he said. Louie nodded in agreement.

He looked like he'd said enough. "Sure thing, boss." He turned to us. "Remember, this was all very, very boring!" He climbed into the passenger seat. Lars revved up the engine and they sped away, around the other side of the mountain.

"That's it! I'm going after them!" Keisha said. She hopped into the Desert Rover and cranked the ignition.

"I'll come with you!" Fernando said. "You three stay here and look for evidence!"

"Roger that!" I said. Fernando hopped in the dune buggy's passenger seat. Then Keisha hit the accelerator, and the two of them sped off.

———⟫◈⟪———

From **Truffle Trouble**
The Case of the Fungus among Us

It had been pretty smart of Mr. Cloulez to hide in the treetops when Madame Lafinque was trying to find him. But it wasn't smart of him at all to get stuck—especially now that a bunch of angry people were making their way in our direction. PJ shimmied up the tree and started untying Mr. Cloulez's shoelace. Derek, Max, and I braced ourselves for their arrival. As they got closer, we heard them chanting "VA T'EN, CLAUDE CLOULEZ!" . . .

"What are they saying?" Max asked.

"Go away, Claude Cloulez," Derek told him.

"They're carrying torches!" Max exclaimed.

"Those are flashlights, Max," Derek said.

The mob reached the top of the driveway where we were standing, and came to a stop. All told, there were probably two or three dozen people. One of the men in front addressed us in English.

"We have come to chase Claude Cloulez out of town," he said angrily. "Step aside!"

The mob roared in agreement.

"It was bad enough when the curse interfered with our crops and our health. But when you brought the curse into the bistro today, you ruined my lunch! That I cannot accept!"

"Don't you know there's no such thing as a curse?" Derek asked in his usual stubborn fashion.

"Not true," said an old woman. "We have recorded the suffering caused by this family for hundreds of years: The Fire of 1798. The Avalanche of 1836. The chronic heartburn epidemic of 1978!"

"Are you sure the Cloulez family was responsible for those things?" Derek asked.

"Absolutely," said a young man. "Things were fine the last few years with no Cloulez people around. But the day Mr. Cloulez returned, my girlfriend broke up with me! And I was diagnosed with incurable bad breath!"

The crowd murmured in horror and sympathy.

"Hmm," Derek said thoughtfully. "Don't you think she broke up with you because of your breath?"

"What are you saying?" the young man shouted. "That is ridiculous! The Cloulez curse is the source of all our woes!"

The crowd rumbled with anger again.

"You can't reason with them, Derek," Max said under his breath.

"He's right," I whispered.

"Tell us where Cloulez is," the first man said. "That's all we want to know."

I was about to invite the mob to look for Mr. Cloulez in the house, since it was now completely dark and both he and PJ were safely out of sight up in the tree. But just then, PJ or Mr. Cloulez slipped, and a small branch broke off and fell to the ground.

Immediately, the group shined their flashlights into the tree. PJ and Mr. Cloulez were hanging in the branches like a pair of frightened raccoons.

"There he is! Get him!" the young man cried. The crowd rushed to surround the base of the tree.

From Snow Problem:
The Case of the Mushing Madness

We scrambled out of the igloo as fast as we could, but we were too late. The sled, with Arnold barely holding on, was already a hundred yards down the road. The dogs ran at full speed, howling happily while Arnold bounced wildly on the rear runner. As the sled disappeared around a bend in the trail, we could hear him yelling, "Where are the brakes?"

Then Fernando jumped on the KC Snow Tracker. He shouted to the rest of us in a take-charge voice . . .

"Curtis, Megan, you guys stay behind. Maybe the dogs'll come back when they're tired or hungry." He pointed to the seat behind him on the Snow Tracker. "Keisha . . . ? C'mon with me. Arnold might need help."

There was no time to argue. Curtis ripped into his back-pack and tossed me one of the Can-Do Communicators. I think he was glad to stay behind. Not that I was surprised—as I said, he's not much for the great outdoors.

I admit I was pretty nervous. With the crazed look in Fernando's eyes, I was afraid he'd suddenly decide he was a stunt man, too, and steer us off a cliff or something. But, I had a mission to accomplish, so I jumped onto the Tracker. "Sure you know what you're doing?" I asked as we zoomed off.

"Yeah, don't worry. My cousin in Blizzard Creek has a snowmobile. We used to race all the time!" I had no chance to second-guess him, or to turn back. Fernando gunned the engine and we burst forward, following the trail left by the dog sled.

I'll give Fernando credit—he knew how to push the Tracker to high speed and still maintain control, even when we hit some rough terrain that nearly bounced us off the machine. After a few minutes, my ears got used to the sound of the engine blasting and the wind racing by.

About the time I decided the ride wasn't so bad, the dogs decided to take a detour off the beaten path. I guess they felt 'the call of the wild,' some primitive urge to head into rougher territory. Suddenly, we veered onto shrubby ground that had plenty of bumps. There were also lots of low-lying branches that nearly smacked us in the face as we sped by. It was hard to keep our eyes on the trail ahead, and on the sled we were chasing. Most of the time, unless the trail stretched out over a long straightaway, we couldn't even see Arnold and the dogs ahead of us. Talk about scary! We never knew what was behind the next curve. Every blind twist was a possible disaster.

We saw the sled take to a narrow road through a small grove of spruce. They were howling pretty fiercely, which should have told us something was up. Fernando revved the engine and followed. Then, just as we whipped around a blind corner, I saw a dark shape step into the trail ahead of us. A moose!

It was huge! Probably seven feet tall, with a giant rack of antlers that reached out at least four feet across. It stood like a brick wall right in the path of our roaring snowmobile. "Fernando!" I screamed. "Moose!" (Like he didn't know.)

There was no time to stop and nowhere else to steer. Unless we wanted to smack into a spruce tree instead, we were gonna hit the side of that moose like a freight train.

———⟫◆⟪———

From Hot-Tempered Farmers:
The Case of the Barbecued Barns

"Hey Megan," Derek said as they tromped across twigs and leaves and a few fallen apples, "are you sure this is the right way? It seems like we've been walking for half an hour."

"Hold on, Derek," she said, squatting down and breaking into an excited whisper. "We've found it. Look over there!"

Derek crouched down beside Megan and peered in the direction she pointed. Through the last few rows of trees, they could see a young man with a ponytail and a tie-dyed T-shirt. He was squatting down beside an old barn. From Mrs. McDog's brief description, they knew it had to be the Apple Barn. It was big and red and had a huge front door shaped like an apple. About a hundred yards off to the right, just like Mrs. McDog had said, they could also make out the pile of ashes that used to be the family's Ultra Comfort Suite.

"What's he doing?" Megan whispered.

"I'm not sure," Derek replied. "It looks like he's trying to drill a stick into that board."

Megan furrowed her eyebrows in that way she does when she's confused.

"Is that some kind of dairy farmer thing?" she asked.

Derek shrugged his shoulders. "Don't ask me. I'm from the city. I get milk from the supermarket."

Megan was about to say something else, but was cut off when the young man started to shout excitedly.

"All right! Finally!"

Megan and Derek watched wide-eyed as he put his stick down and began to fan a small flame with his hands!

"Derek!" Megan whispered as loud as she dared. "It really is an arsonist! Just look at him! He's come back to torch another barn!"

"Fire!" the young man cried out as the flames began to grow. "Yeeeee-Hah!"

"He's setting the Apple Barn on fire!" Megan continued. "We've got to stop him!"

———⇒•◇•⇐———

From **Metal Heads:**
The Case of the Rival Robots

Marci turned the main controls on and Emma twisted the joystick on the remote. The lights blinked on around Muggsy's middle and we all cheered.

"Muggsy's back!" I yelled.

And then . . . nothing.

"C'mon, Emma, get him going," said Marci. "Give him the juice."

Emma twisted the joystick frantically. "I *am* telling him to move. He's still not working."

Muggsy stood, frozen in place. The blinking lights were his only signs of life.

PJ took the basketball and rolled it gently toward Muggsy. It bounced lazily off him, and rolled away to a stop.

Marci sighed, looking down at the floor. Emma twisted the joystick around and around, as if refusing to believe it wouldn't work. The Thompson twins sighed in perfect unison. And Katie blew a big, fat, purple bubble.

I looked at the other members of the Super Crew, and then at the big clock on the scoreboard. It was less than an hour to Muggsy's spot in the contest. Now that we'd removed what we thought was the problem, we had no idea what could be wrong with him.

From One Norse Town:
The Case of the Suspicious Scrolls

I trotted over to help Max. When I picked up a thick textbook called *Medieval Norse History*, I saw something that caught me completely off guard. The book had fallen open, face-down, and when I lifted it up, there was a pile of money underneath it. And we're not talking spare change—we're talking bunches of crisp one-hundred-dollar bills!

I turned the book over and saw that someone had carved a big hole in all of the pages, leaving a space to stash the cash. I had no idea what the money was for, but it looked like Max's stomach had led us to our first clue.

"Hey, Crew," I said, trying not to speak too loudly. "Get over here *now*! Look at what's in this book!" I showed them the carved-out pages and the wads of hundreds.

"There must be ten or twenty thousand dollars here!" said PJ, flipping through the bills with amazement.

Up until now, everything had looked pretty normal on the museum's end. But how could we explain *this*?

⟫◆⟪

From **Rock the House:**
The Case of the Meteorite Menace

"Whoa!" Megan yelled. "We've been hit!"

Bang! Another one.

"What is going on?" Megan yelled again. "It's like those meteorites are aiming for us!"

It was bizarre all right, but I wasn't worried about getting hurt. The X-100's roof has triple-reinforced titanium plates. There was no way those falling rocks could get to us. At least until Max leaped to our rescue.

"I'll activate the force field!" he screamed out, lurching for the control panel.

"Max!" I yelled, trying to stop him. "We don't even have a force field." Too late. He flipped one of the switches closest to ALEC's keyboard. The result was immediate. A big section of the ceiling slid open. The train's P.A. system came on to announce what was up.

"Activating sun roof now," it said in its cold, robotic voice. "Enjoy the sunshine!"

"Uh oh," Max said.

"Close it, Max!" Megan screamed. "Now!"

Too late. The thing we all most feared finally happened.

There was an ear-splitting bang as a meteorite fell into the Control Car! The rock had caught the side of the control panel, missing Max by less than four feet. Max was fine, but the impact had activated one of the control panel switches.

"Activating thruster rockets now," the train's voice announced.

WWWHHHOOOSSSHHH!!!

The rockets fired. The sudden acceleration knocked all four of us back against the Control Car door. I don't know if you've ever seen a drag race, but the KC Express Train would've left any dragster choking in our dust. Cold, wet air blew in our faces as we tore down the side of the hill like some kind of wild roller-coaster ride of no return.

━━▷◆◁━━

NOW HEAR THIS!!

Every week tune in to the Kinetic City Super Crew radio show!

If you think reading about the Crew is cool,
wait till you hear them blasting out of your radio.
Every week the Super Crew find themselves tangled up
in danger and mystery in a different place...
from the icy tundras of Alaska to the busy
streets of Kinetic City.

Call 1-800-877-CREW (2739)

to find out where you can tune in to hear
the next awesome episode of
Kinetic City Super Crew.

KCSC is featured on Aahs World Radio and finer public radio stations around the country.

 AMERICAN ASSOCIATION FOR THE ADVANCEMENT OF SCIENCE   National Science Foundation

Check out
Kinetic City Cyber Club
a science mystery game
on the World Wide Web

Come and Play!
http://www.kineticcity.com

How would you like to try solving your own mystery with the Super Crew? It's waiting for you now, at Kineticcity.com!

You'll also find games, info on your favorite Super Crew members, online chats, and cool things to download, like stationery and screen savers. There's even a page for teachers and parents.

When you get to the site make sure you bookmark it. You'll want to go there every day because there's always something new and fun happening at Kinetic City Cyber Club!

AMERICAN ASSOCIATION FOR THE
ADVANCEMENT OF SCIENCE

National Science Foundation

The staff of the Kinetic City Super Crew Radio Project:

Executive Producer:	Bob Hirshon
Senior Producer:	Joe Shepherd
Producer/Engineer:	Barnaby Bristol
Assistant Producer:	Anna Ewald
Director:	Susan Keady
Writers:	Chuck Harwood
	Marianne Meyer
	Sara St. Antoine
	Justin Warner
Associate Editor:	Samantha Beres
The Crew:	Damion Connor
	Elana Eisen-Markowitz
	Joaquin Foster-Gross
	Reggie Harris
	Melody Johnson
	Monique McClung
	Jennifer Roberts
	Paul Simon
Business Manager:	Thu Vu
Outreach Coordinator:	Corette Jones
Project Assistant:	Renee Stockdale-Homick
Cyber Club Producer:	Kimberly Amaral
EHR, Head:	Shirley Malcom
Director,	
Public Understanding of Science:	Alan McGowan
Science Content Advisor:	David Lindley
Executive Officer, AAAS:	Richard Nicholson